W9-AVS-305

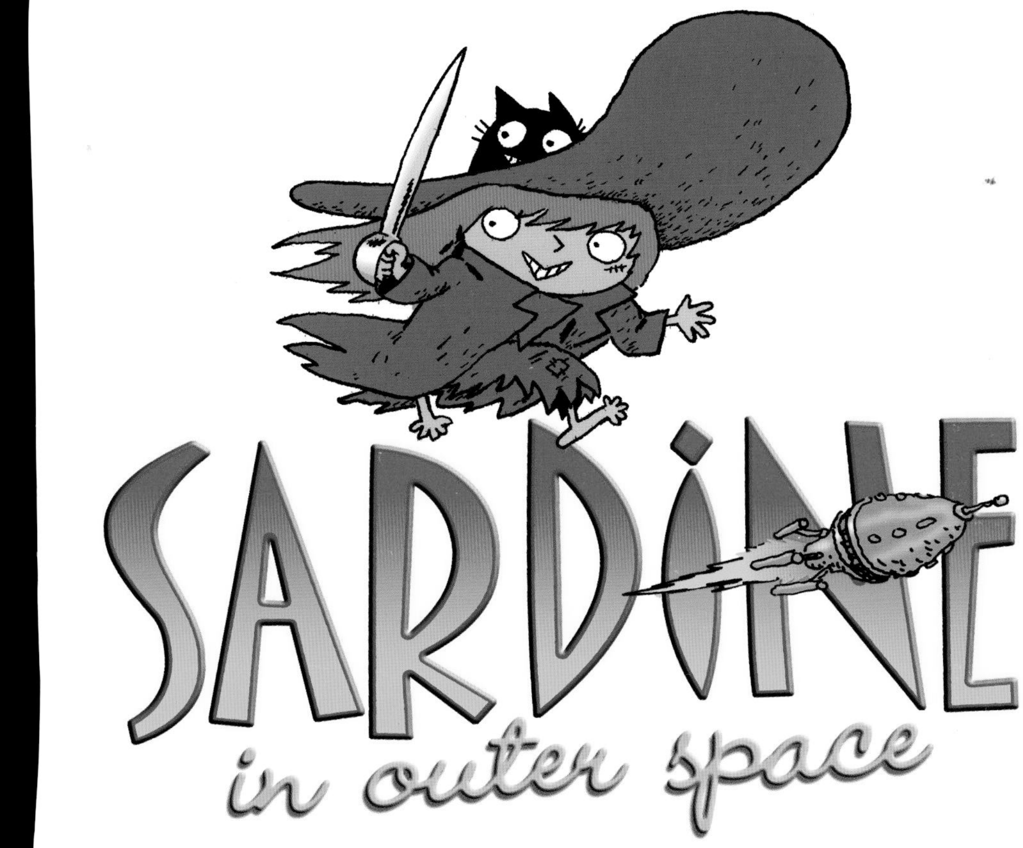

SARDINE
in outer space

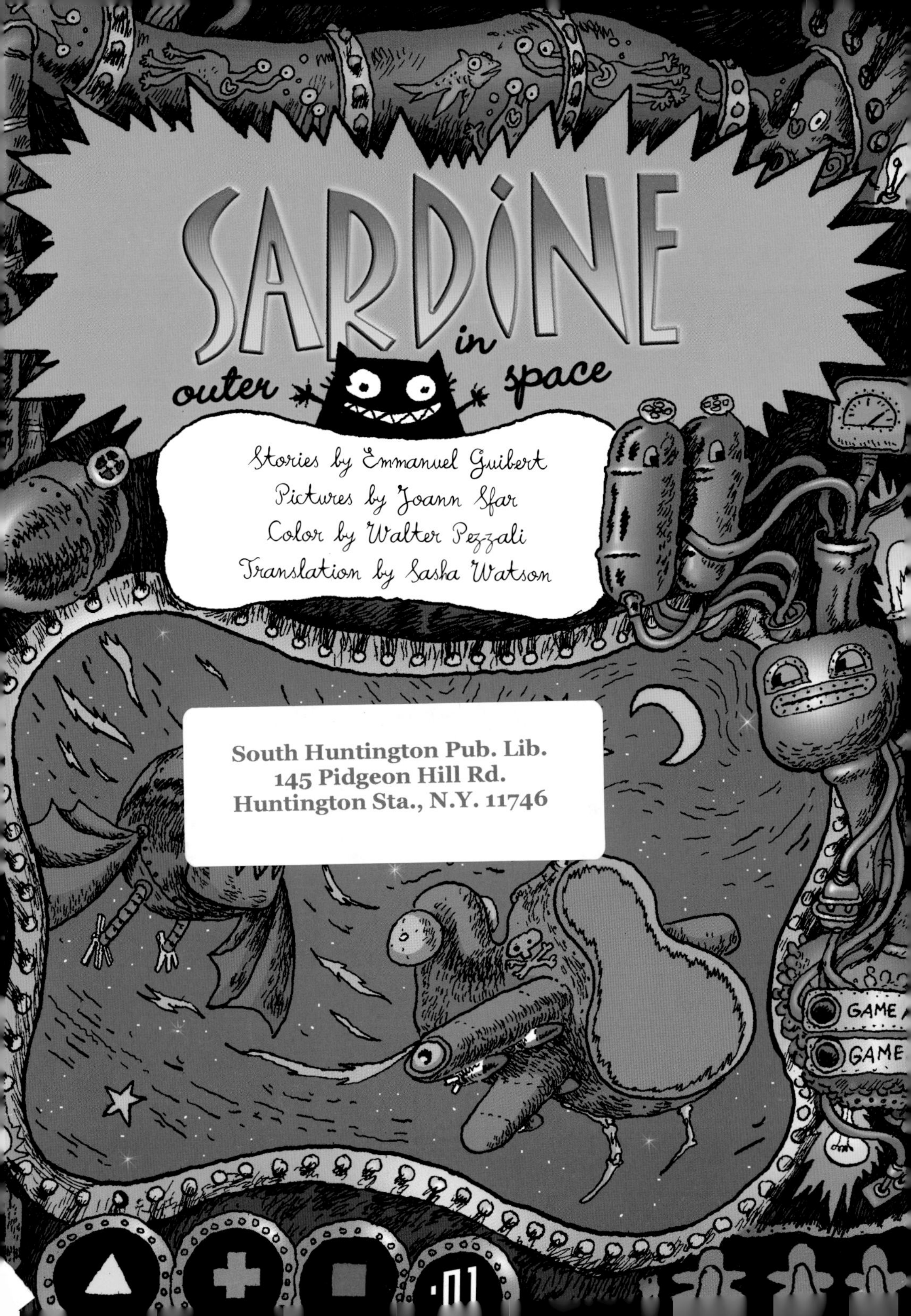
SARDINE
in
outer space
Stories by Emmanuel Guibert
Pictures by Joann Sfar
Color by Walter Pezzali
Translation by Sasha Watson
GAME
GAME

Contents

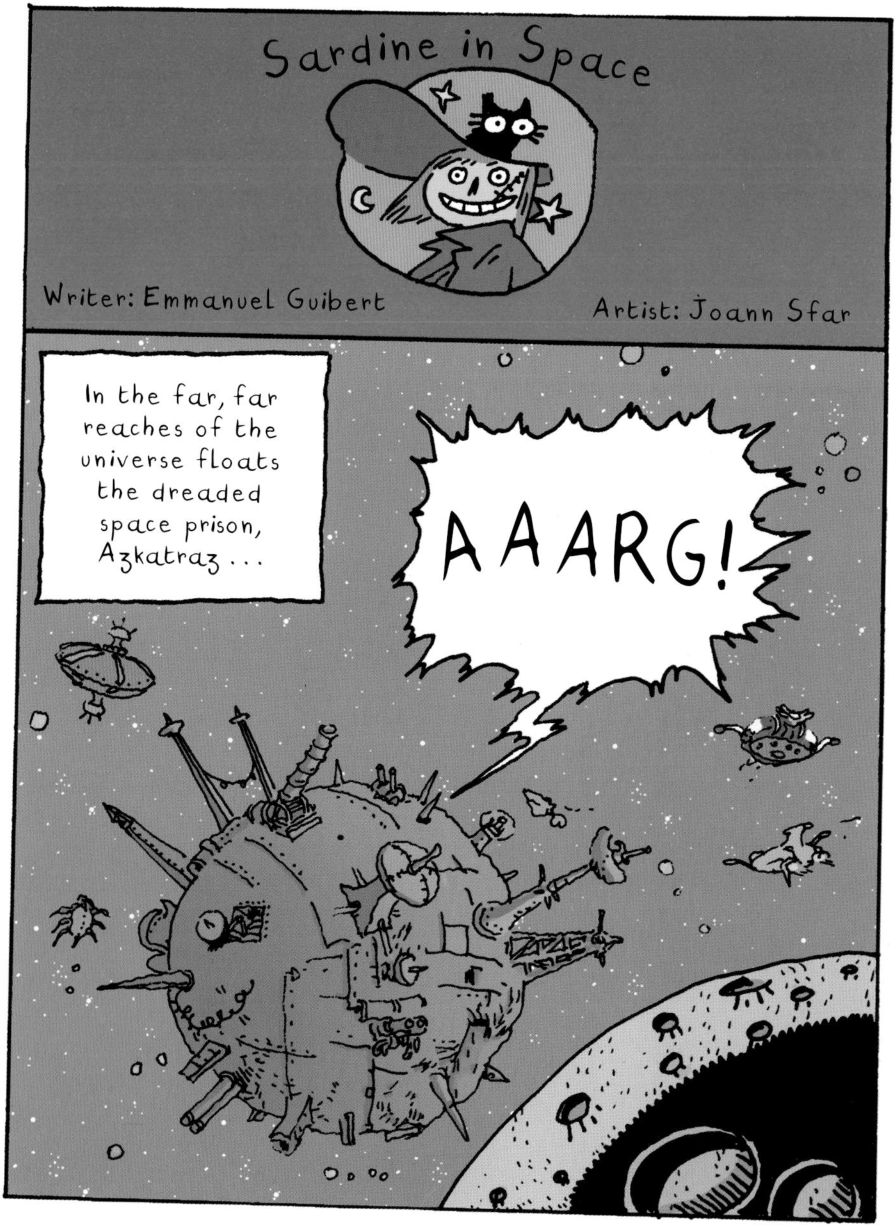
Sardine in Space
Writer: Emmanuel Guibert
Artist: Joann Sfar
In the far, far reaches of the universe floats the dreaded space prison, Azkatraz . . .
AAARG!

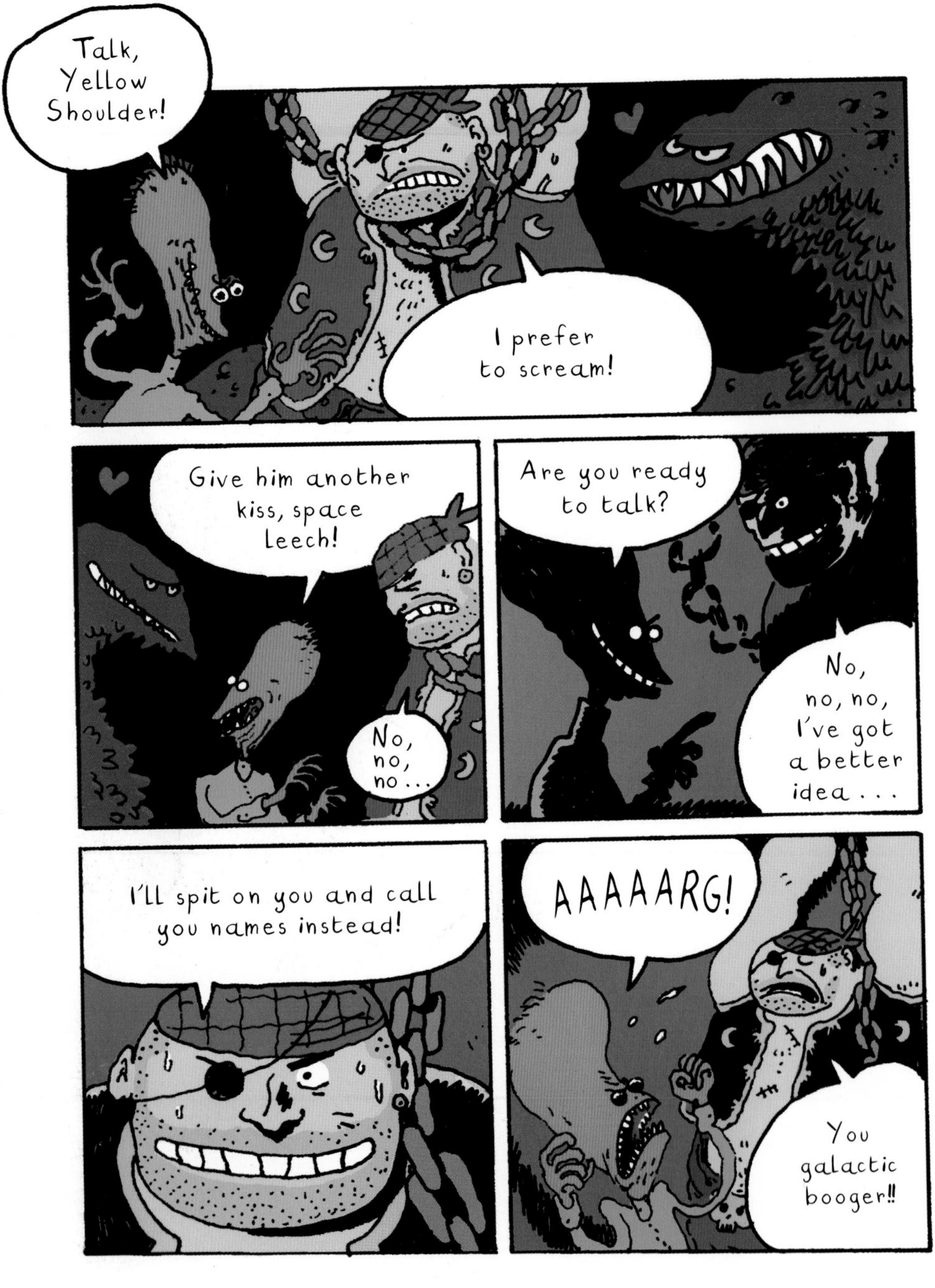
Talk, Yellow Shoulder!
I prefer to scream!
Give him another kiss, space Leech!
No, no, no...
Are you ready to talk?
No, no, no, I've got a better idea...
I'LL spit on you and call you names instead!
AAAAARG!
You galactic booger!!

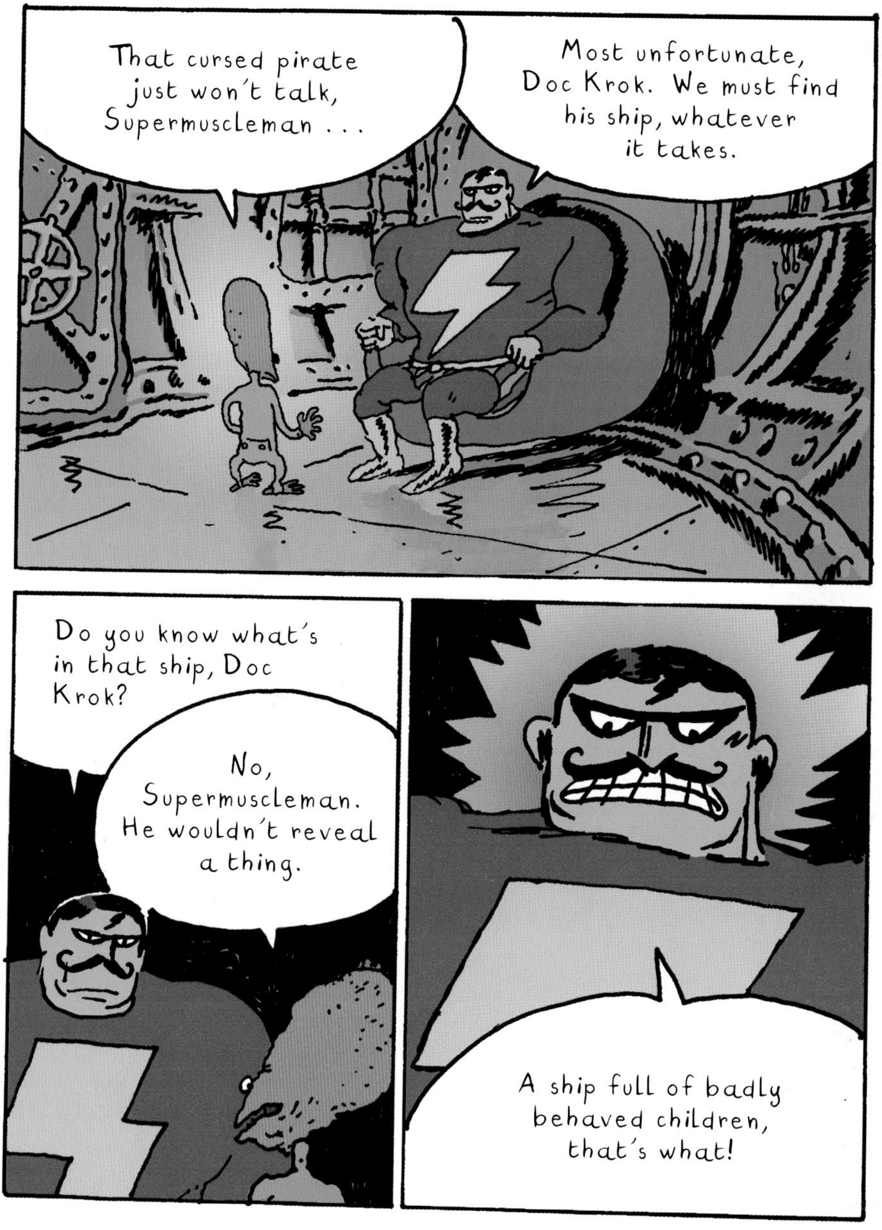
That cursed pirate just won't talk, Supermuscleman . . .
Most unfortunate, Doc Krok. We must find his ship, whatever it takes.
Do you know what's in that ship, Doc Krok?
No, Supermuscleman. He wouldn't reveal a thing.
A ship full of badly behaved children, that's what!

We have trained children throughout the universe to obey us at all times, Doc Krok!

Yes, Super-muscleman.

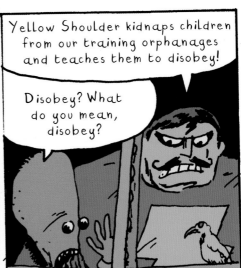

Yellow Shoulder kidnaps children from our training orphanages and teaches them to disobey!

Disobey? What do you mean, disobey?

Disobedience, Doc Krok, is a major threat to us!

Really, Supermuscle-man?

And of all the disobedient children, SHE is the most dangerous!

Oh! She's so cute!

6

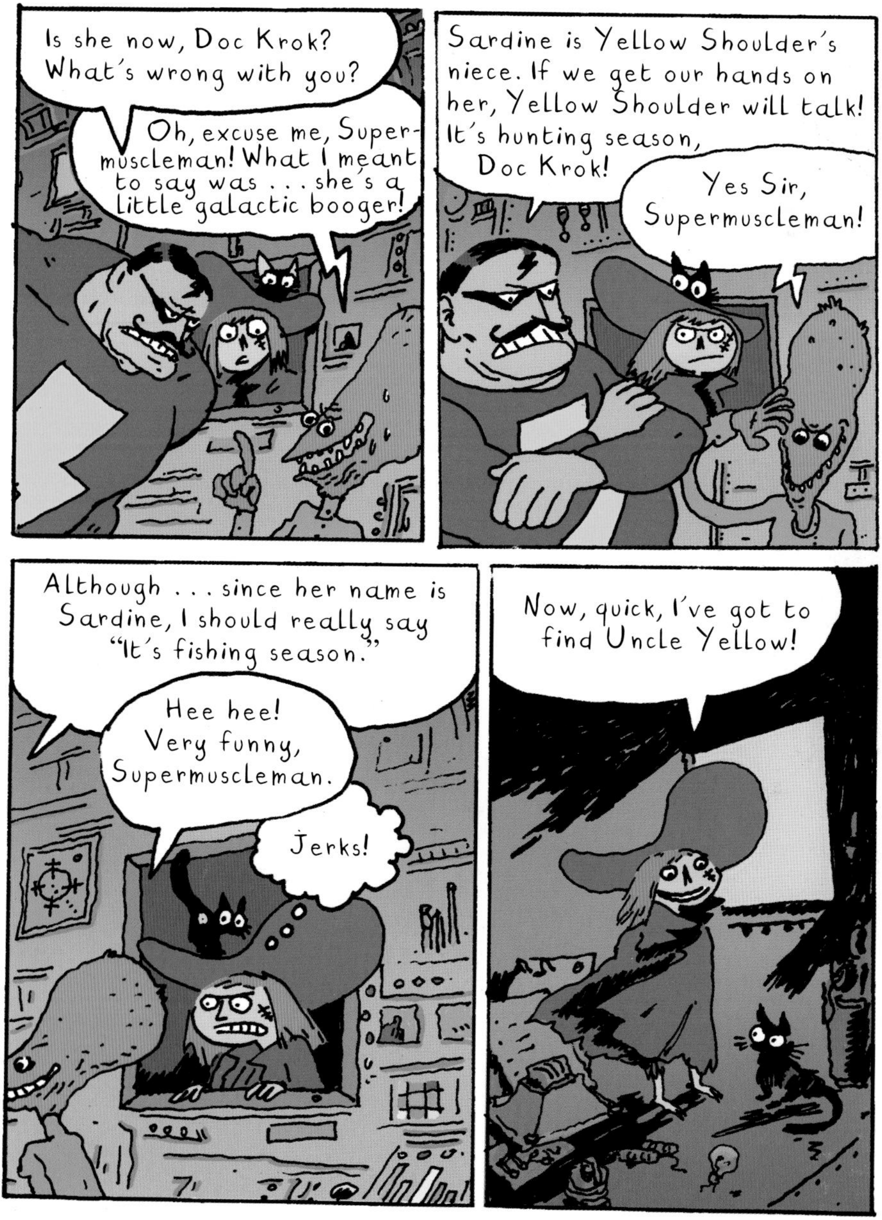
Is she now, Doc Krok? What's wrong with you?
Oh, excuse me, Supermuscleman! What I meant to say was . . . she's a little galactic booger!
Sardine is Yellow Shoulder's niece. If we get our hands on her, Yellow Shoulder will talk! It's hunting season, Doc Krok!
Yes Sir, Supermuscleman!
Although . . . since her name is Sardine, I should really say "It's fishing season."
Hee hee! Very funny, Supermuscleman.
Jerks!
Now, quick, I've got to find Uncle Yellow!

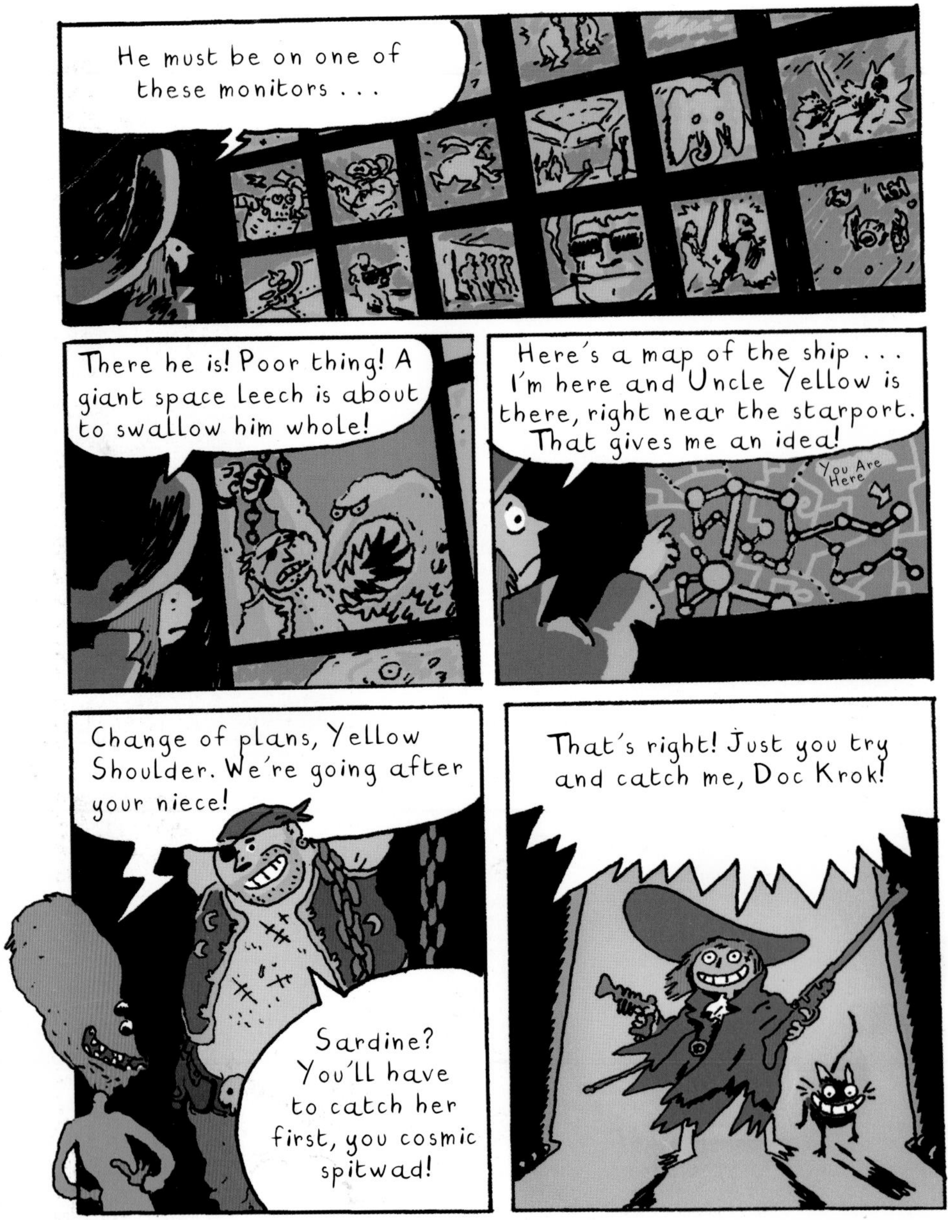
He must be on one of these monitors . . .
There he is! Poor thing! A giant space leech is about to swallow him whole!
Here's a map of the ship . . . I'm here and Uncle Yellow is there, right near the starport. That gives me an idea!
You Are Here
Change of plans, Yellow Shoulder. We're going after your niece!
Sardine? You'll have to catch her first, you cosmic spitwad!
That's right! Just you try and catch me, Doc Krok!

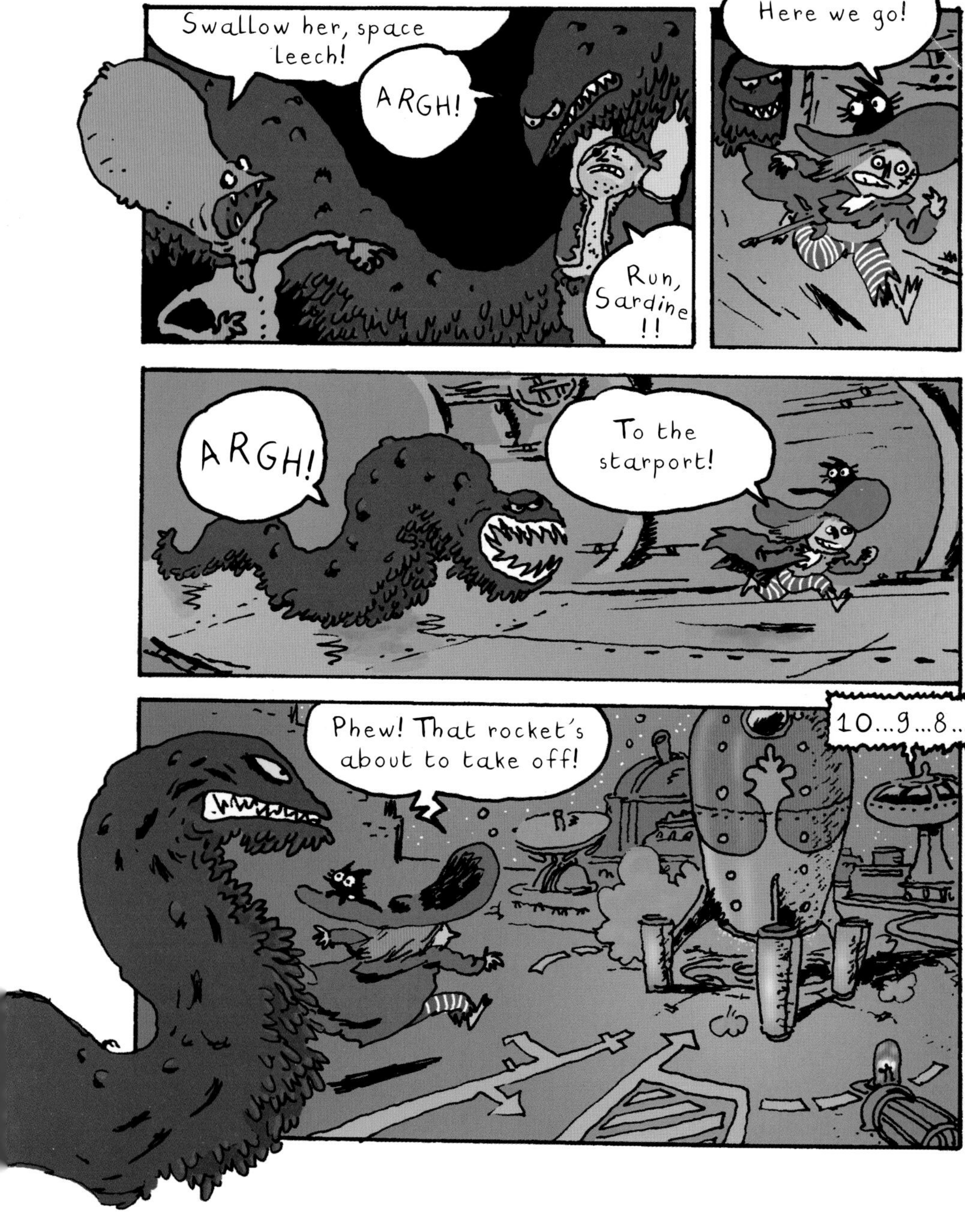

Swallow her, space leech!
ARGH!
Run, Sardine!!
Here we go!
ARGH!
To the starport!
Phew! That rocket's about to take off!
10...9...8...

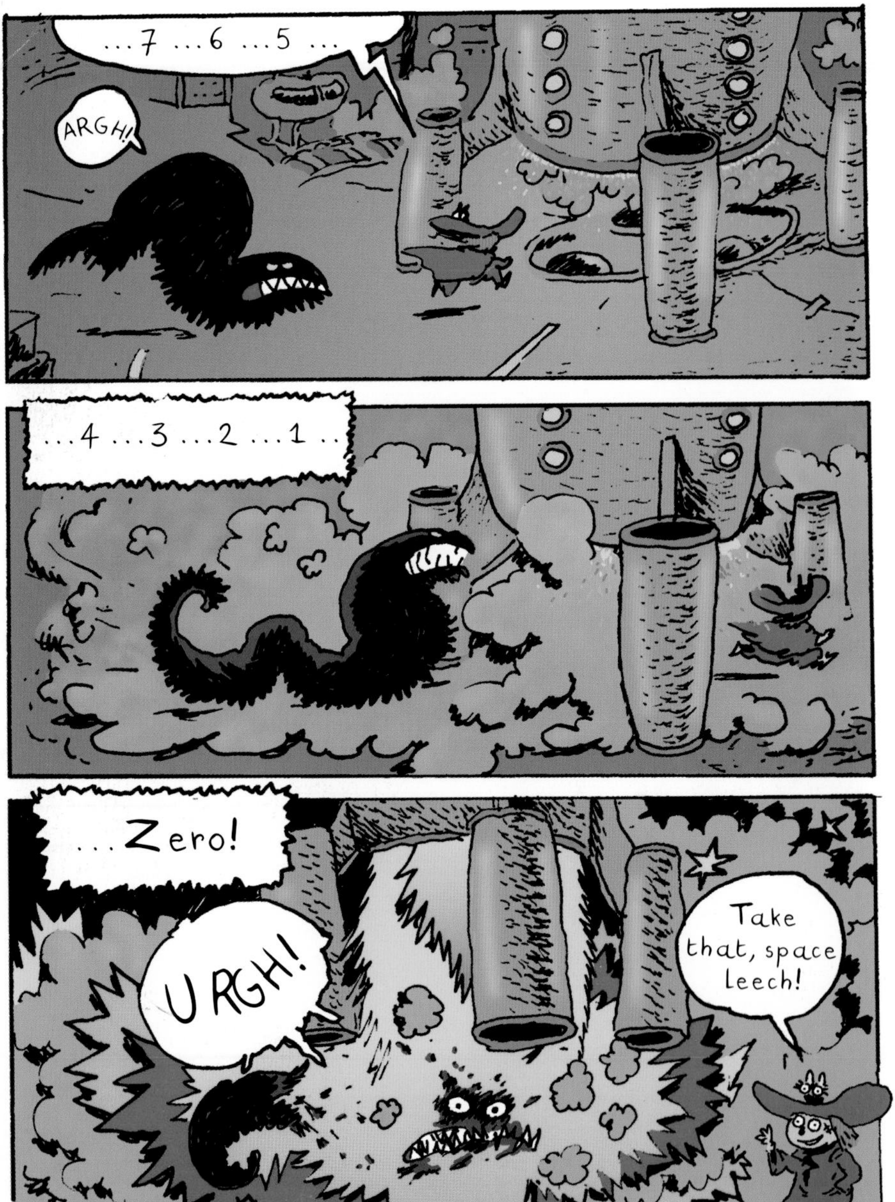

...7 ...6 ...5 ...
ARGH!
...4 ...3 ...2 ...1 ...
...Zero!
URGH!
Take that, space leech!

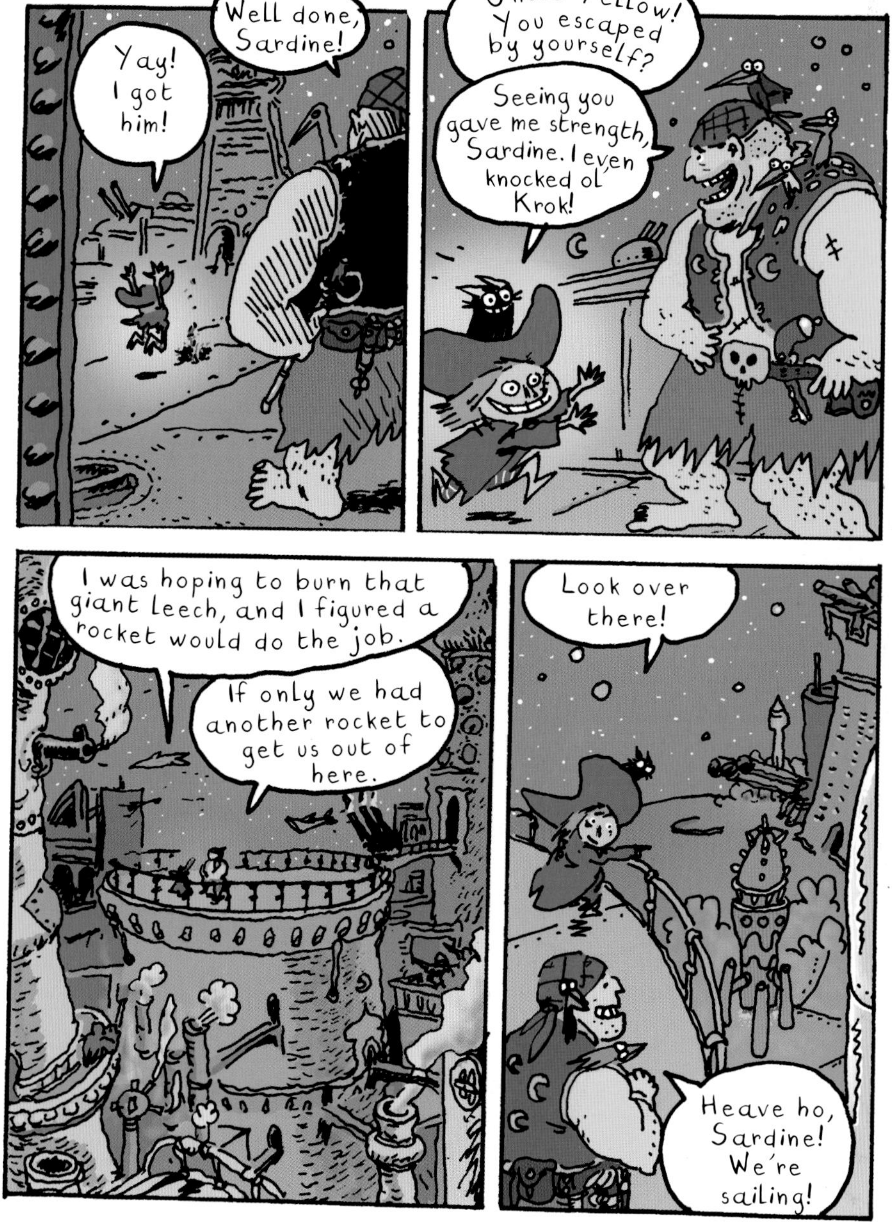
Yay! I got him!
Well done, Sardine!
Uncle Yellow! You escaped by yourself?
Seeing you gave me strength, Sardine. I even knocked ol' Krok!
I was hoping to burn that giant leech, and I figured a rocket would do the job.
If only we had another rocket to get us out of here.
Look over there!
Heave ho, Sardine! We're sailing!

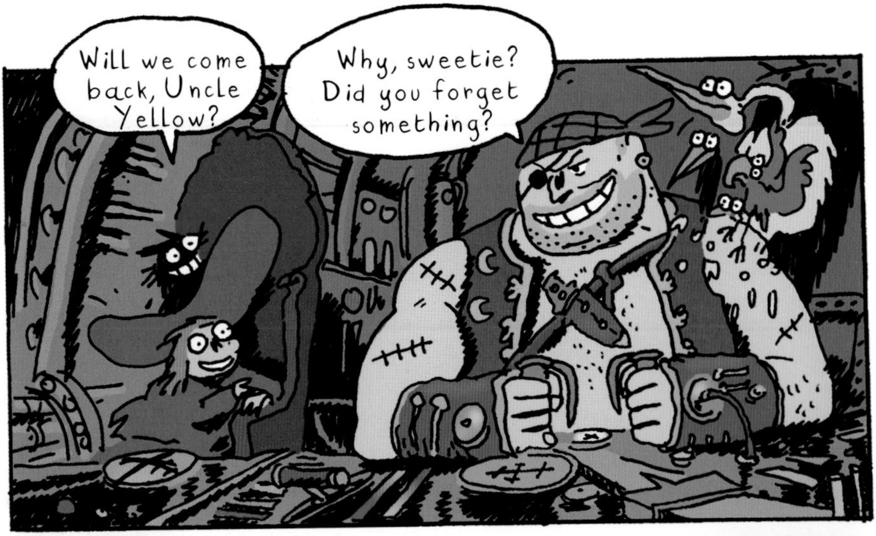
Will we come back, Uncle Yellow?
Why, sweetie? Did you forget something?

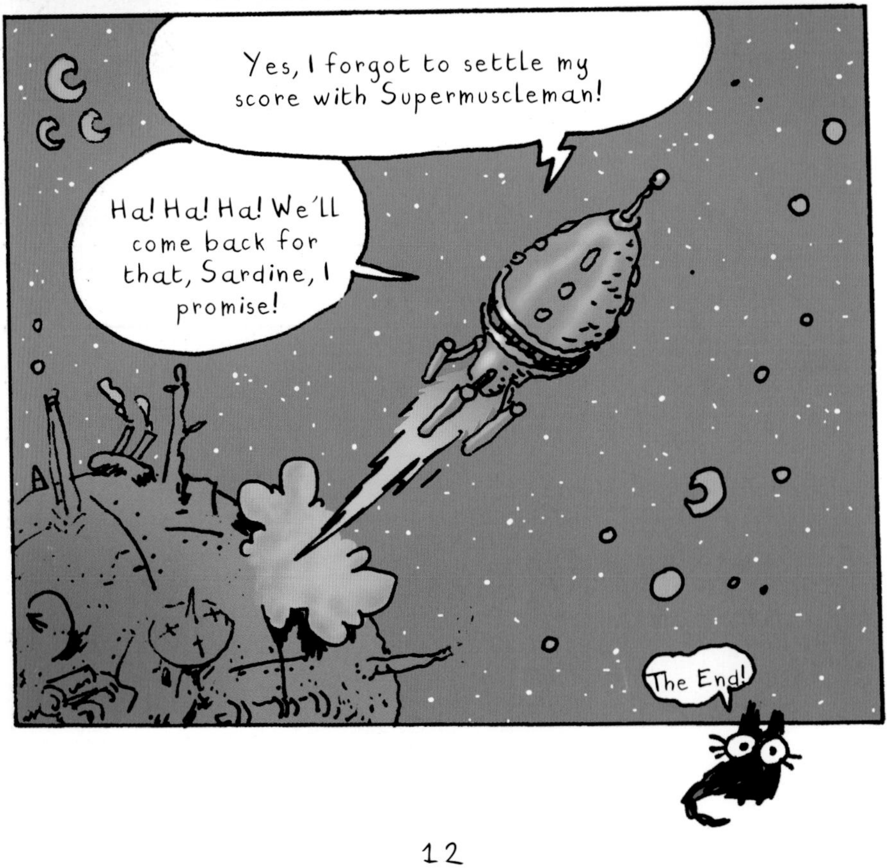
Yes, I forgot to settle my score with Supermuscleman!
Ha! Ha! Ha! We'll come back for that, Sardine, I promise!
The End!

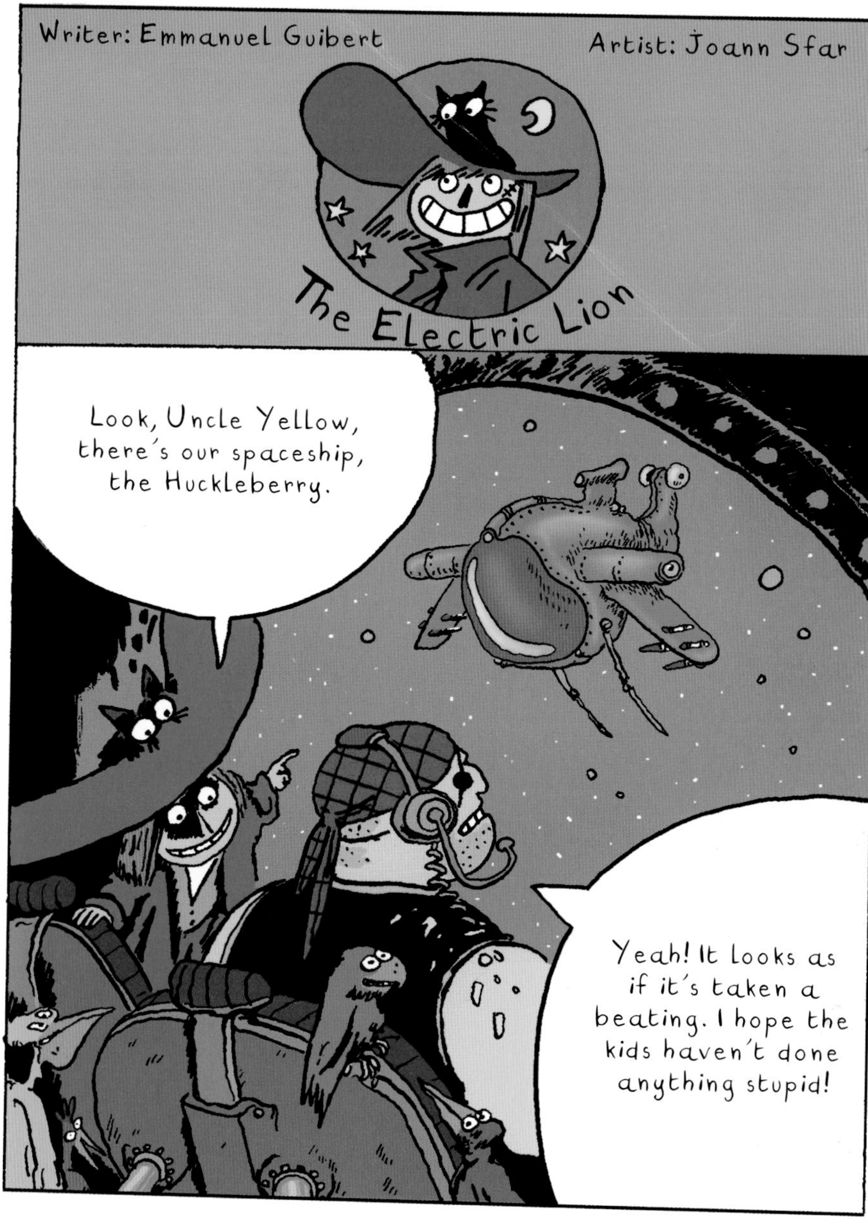
Writer: Emmanuel Guibert
Artist: Joann Sfar
The Electric Lion
Look, Uncle Yellow, there's our spaceship, the Huckleberry.
Yeah! It looks as if it's taken a beating. I hope the kids haven't done anything stupid!

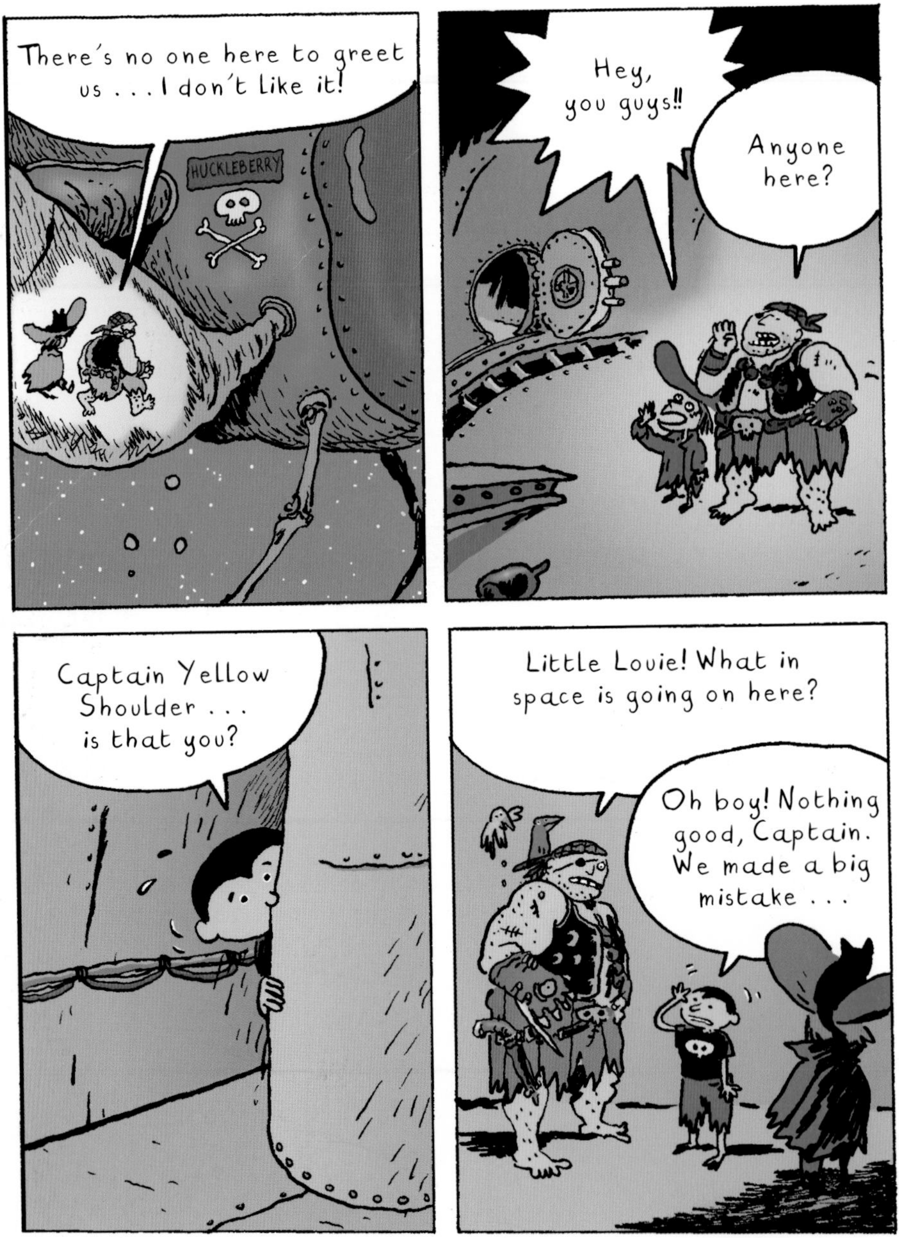
There's no one here to greet us . . . I don't like it!
HUCKLEBERRY
Hey, you guys!!
Anyone here?
Captain Yellow Shoulder . . . is that you?
Little Louie! What in space is going on here?
Oh boy! Nothing good, Captain. We made a big mistake . . .

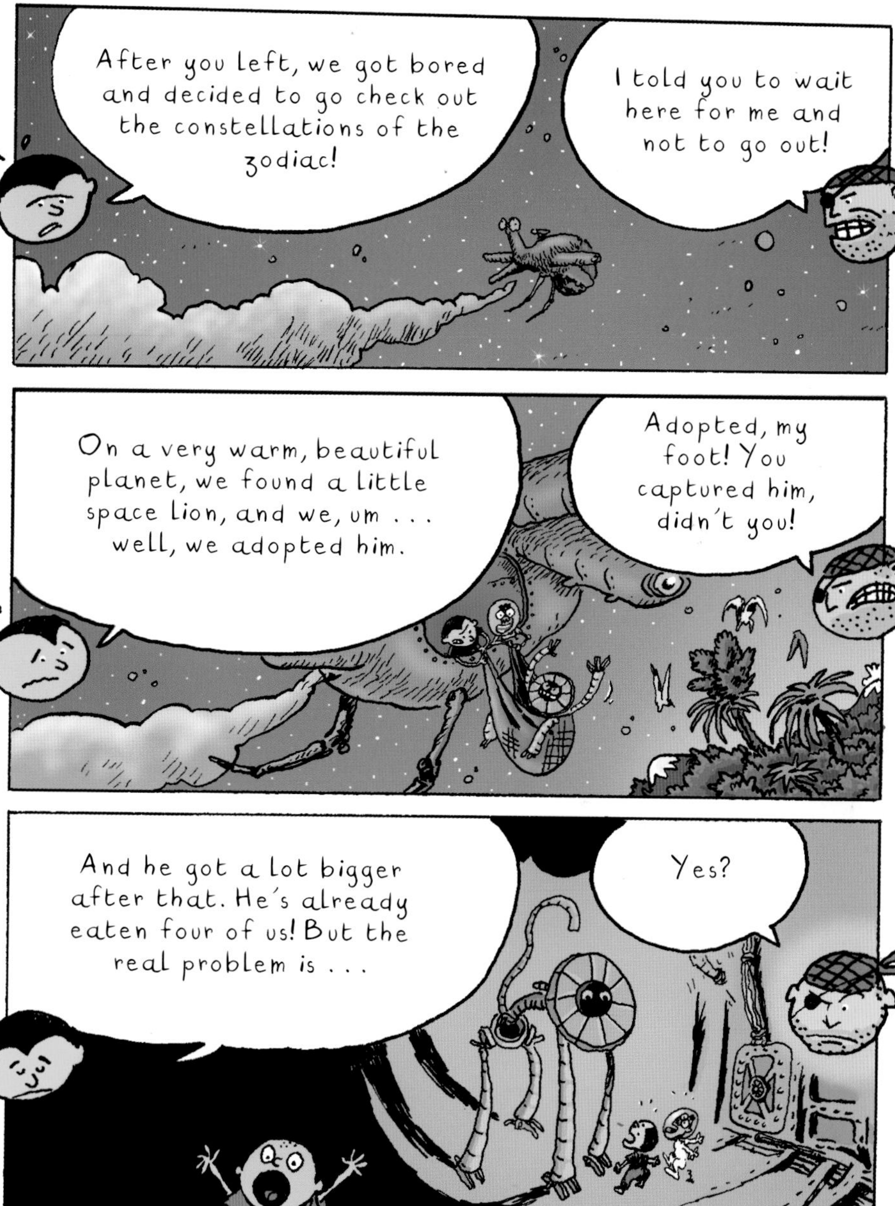
After you left, we got bored and decided to go check out the constellations of the zodiac!
I told you to wait here for me and not to go out!
On a very warm, beautiful planet, we found a little space lion, and we, um . . . well, we adopted him.
Adopted, my foot! You captured him, didn't you!
And he got a lot bigger after that. He's already eaten four of us! But the real problem is . . .
Yes?

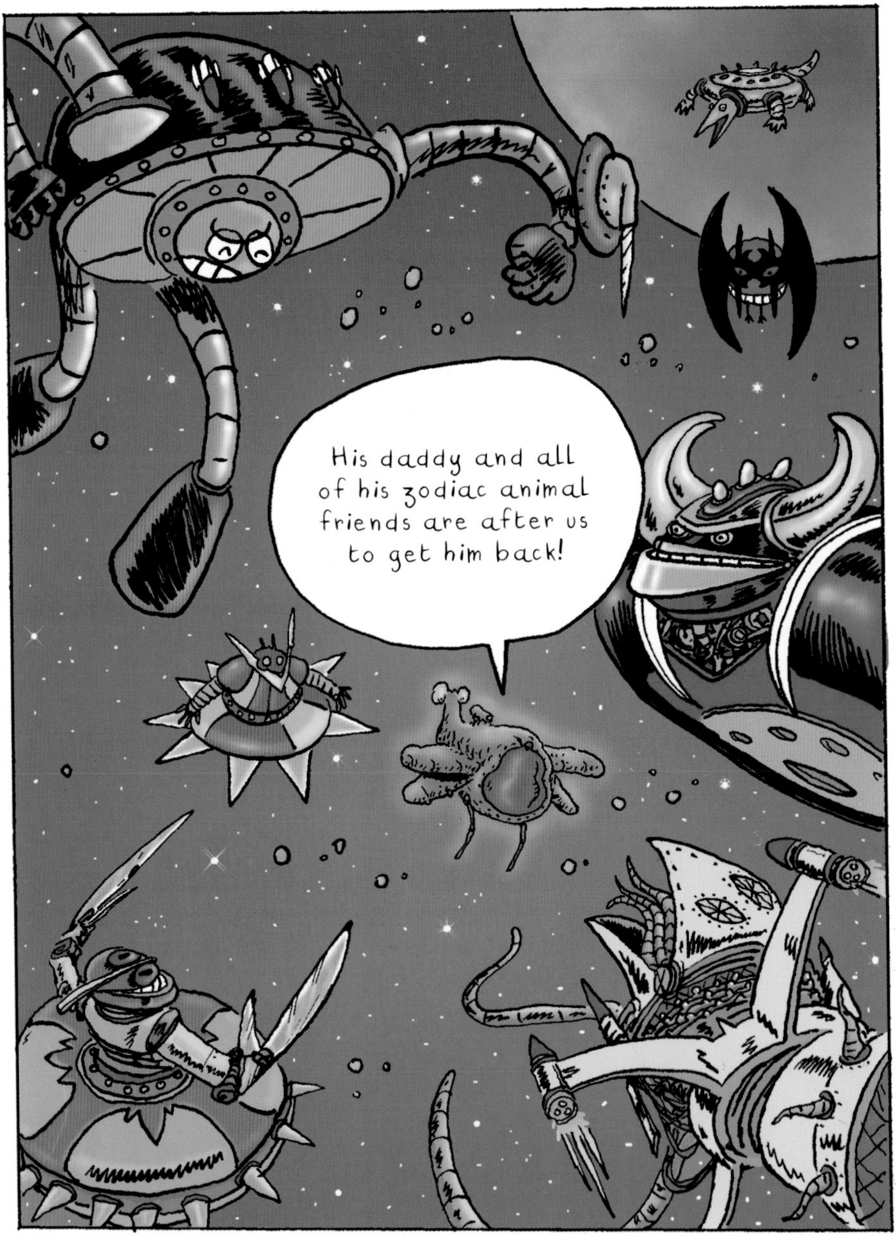
His daddy and all of his zodiac animal friends are after us to get him back!

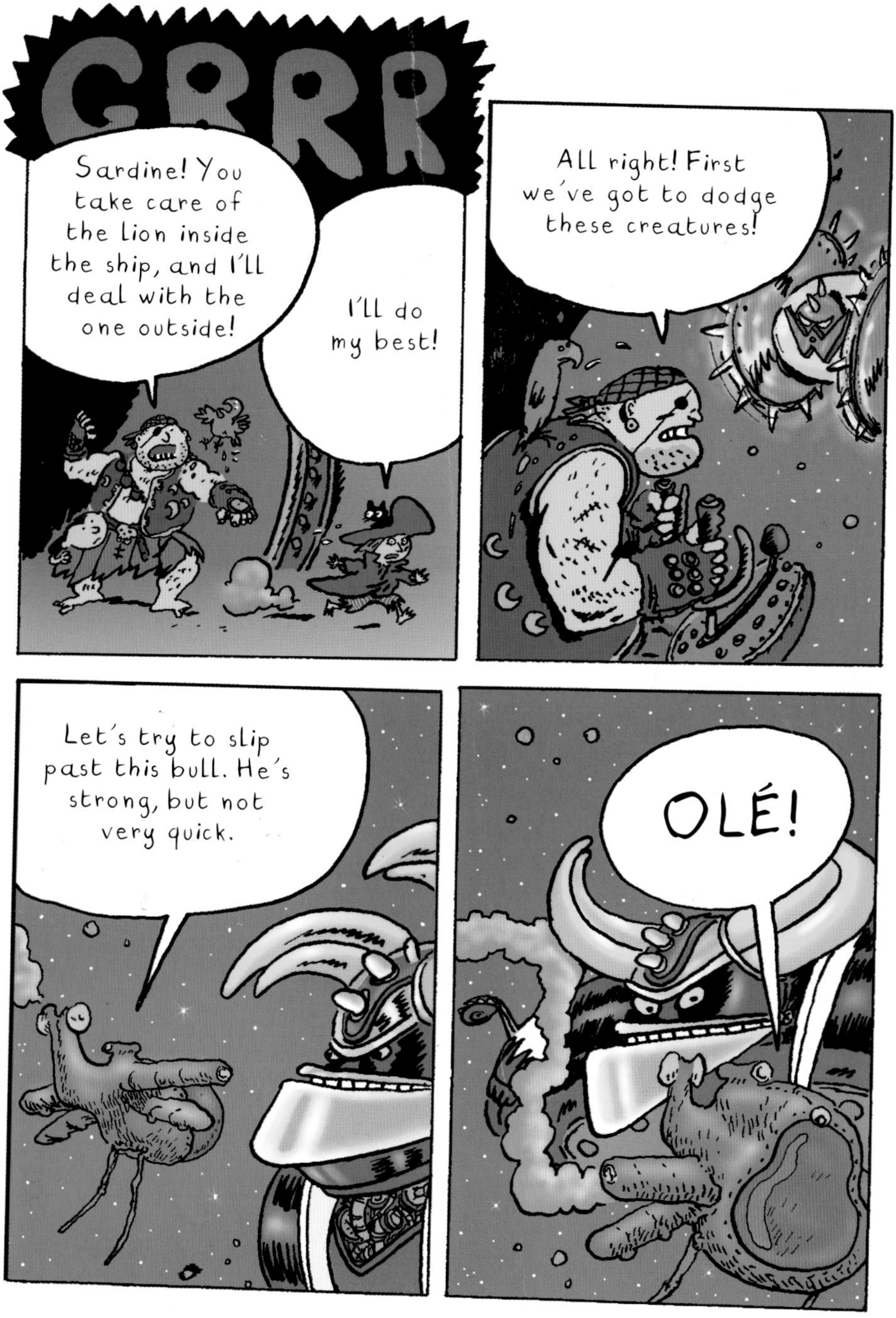
GRRR
Sardine! You take care of the lion inside the ship, and I'll deal with the one outside!
I'll do my best!
All right! First we've got to dodge these creatures!
Let's try to slip past this bull. He's strong, but not very quick.
OLÉ!

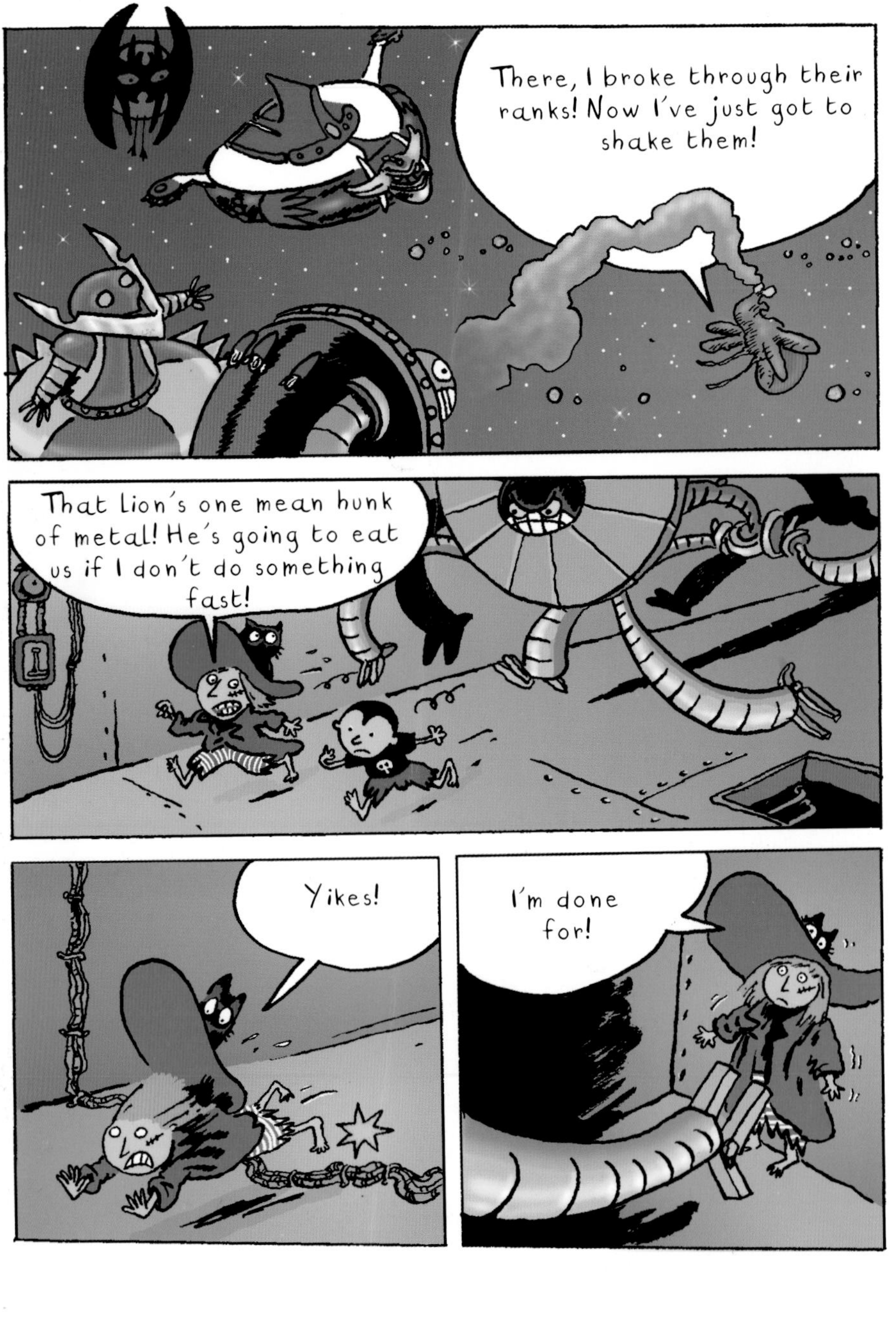
There, I broke through their ranks! Now I've just got to shake them!
That Lion's one mean hunk of metal! He's going to eat us if I don't do something fast!
Yikes!
I'm done for!

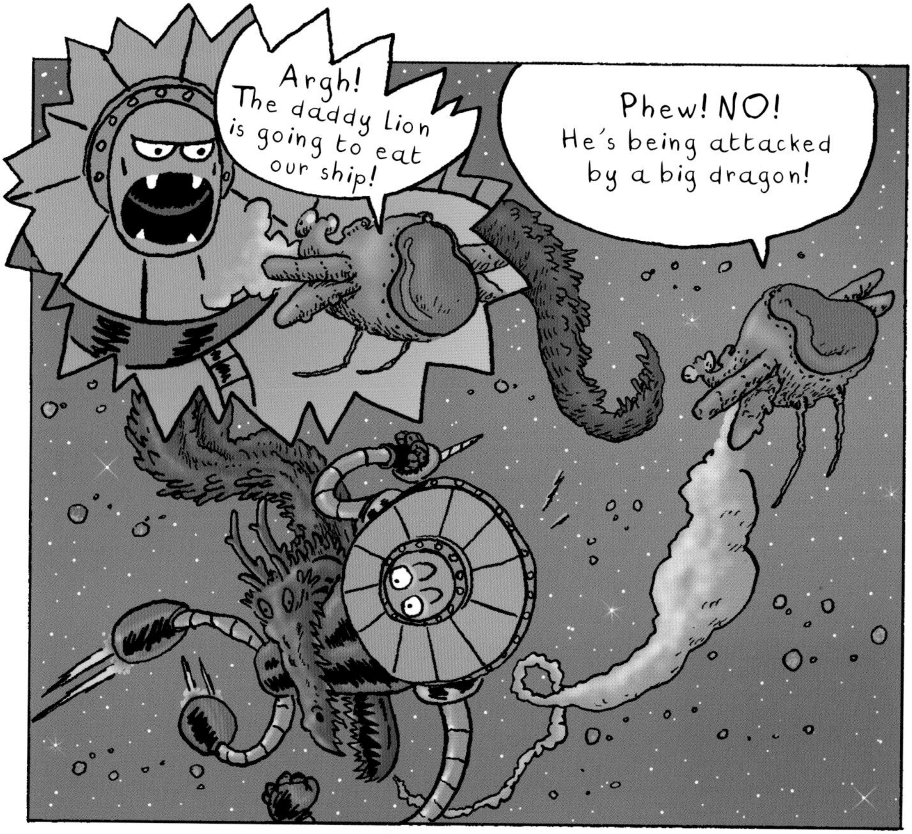
Argh! The daddy lion is going to eat our ship!
Phew! NO! He's being attacked by a big dragon!

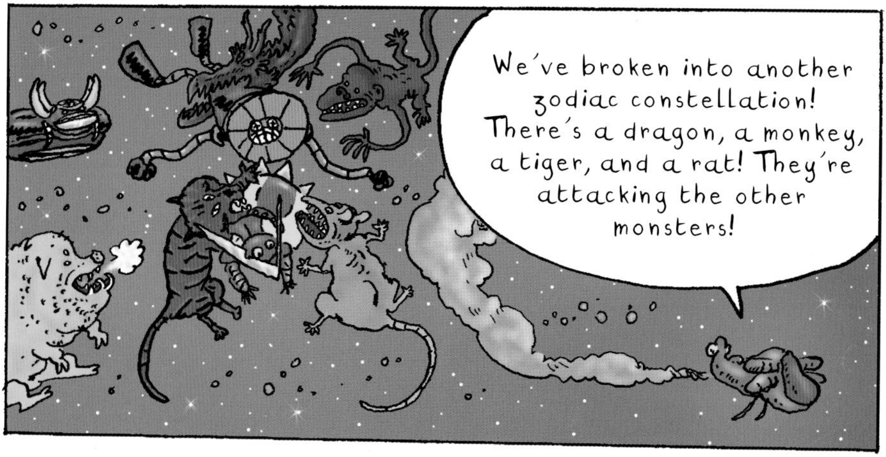
We've broken into another zodiac constellation! There's a dragon, a monkey, a tiger, and a rat! They're attacking the other monsters!

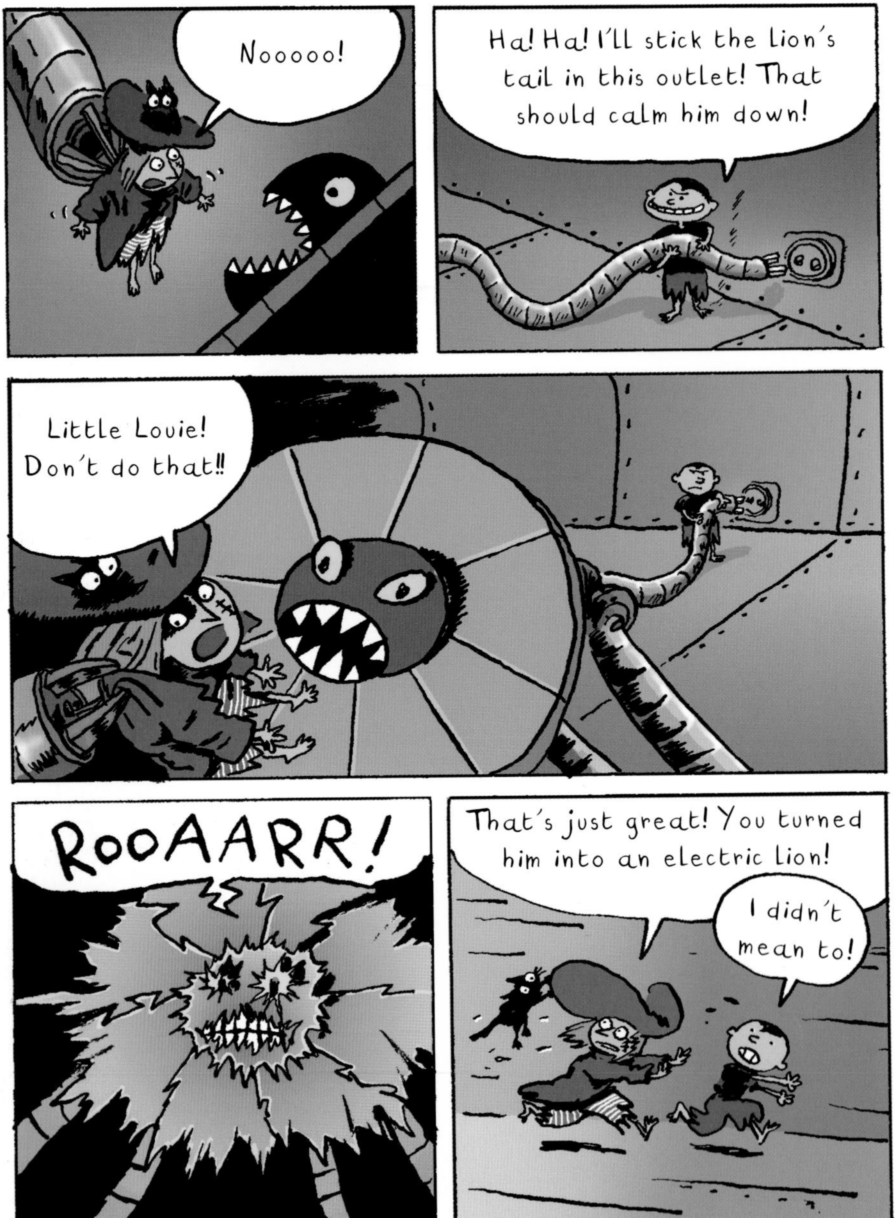
Nooooo!
Ha! Ha! I'll stick the Lion's tail in this outlet! That should calm him down!
Little Louie! Don't do that!!
ROOAARR!
That's just great! You turned him into an electric Lion!
I didn't mean to!

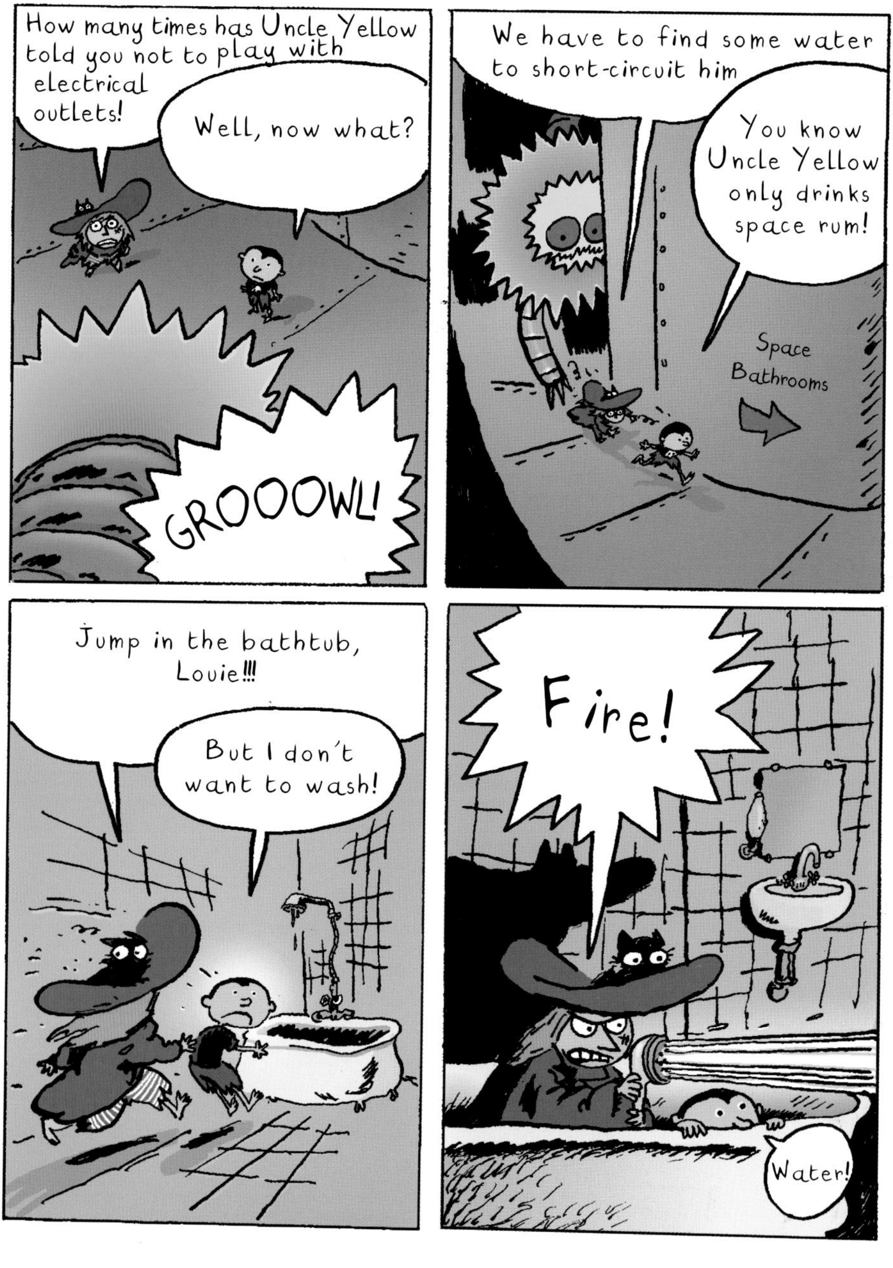
How many times has Uncle Yellow told you not to play with electrical outlets!
Well, now what?
GROOOWL!
We have to find some water to short-circuit him
You know Uncle Yellow only drinks space rum!
Space Bathrooms
Jump in the bathtub, Louie!!!
But I don't want to wash!
Fire!
Water!

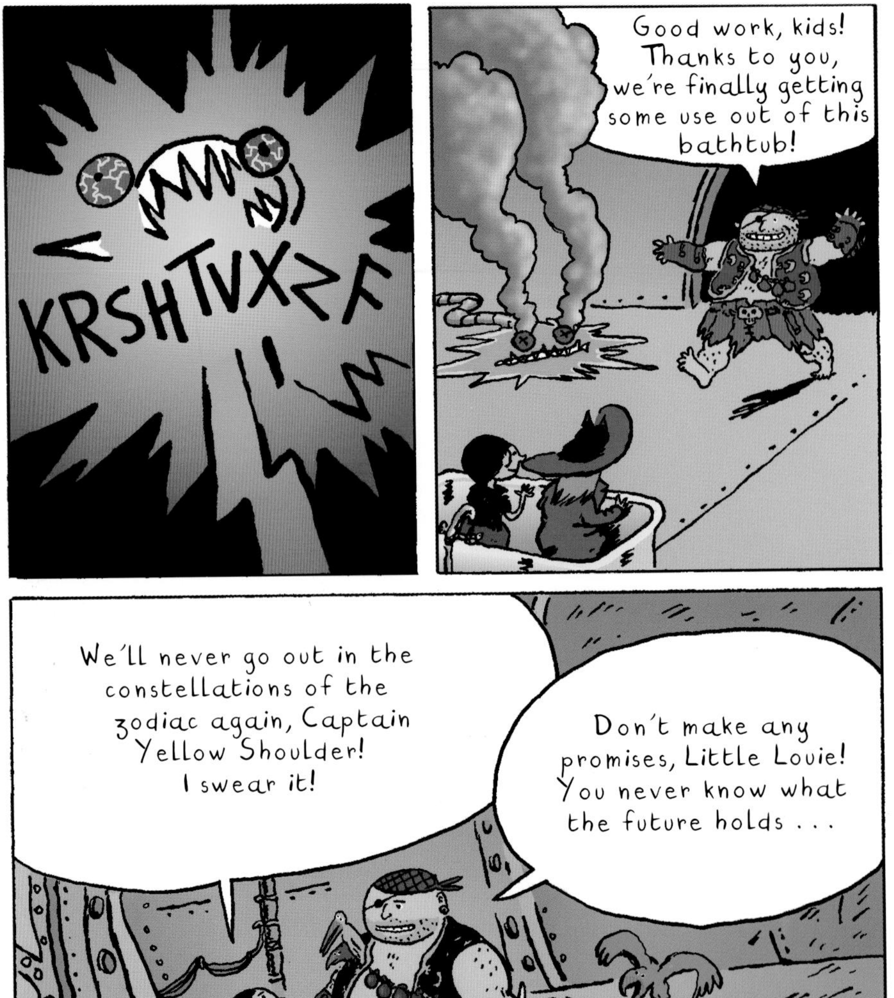
KRSHTVXZF
Good work, kids! Thanks to you, we're finally getting some use out of this bathtub!
We'll never go out in the constellations of the zodiac again, Captain Yellow Shoulder! I swear it!
Don't make any promises, Little Louie! You never know what the future holds . . .
The End

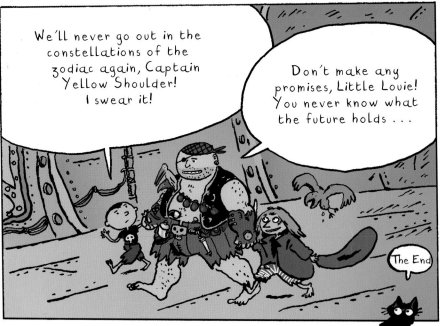

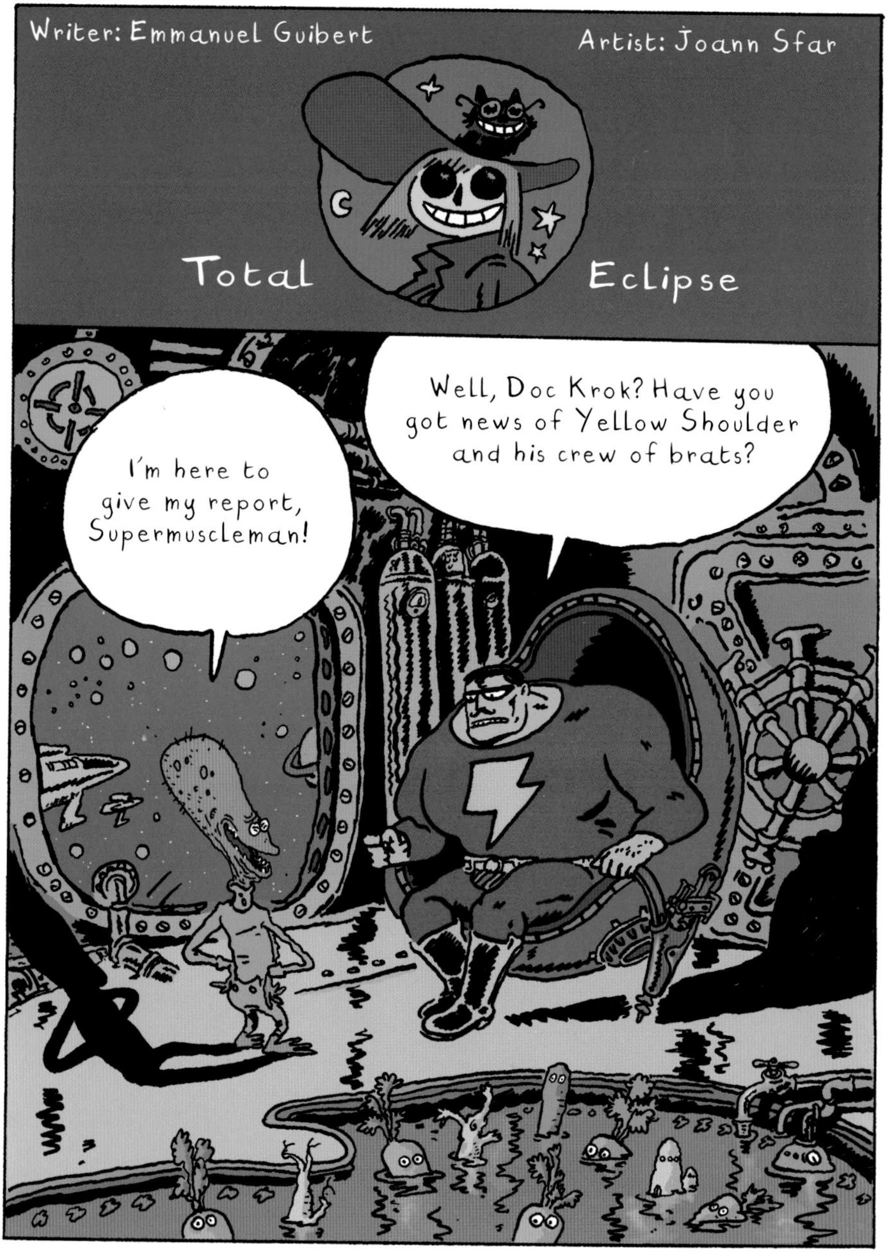
Writer: Emmanuel Guibert
Artist: Joann Sfar
Total Eclipse
I'm here to give my report, Supermuscleman!
Well, Doc Krok? Have you got news of Yellow Shoulder and his crew of brats?

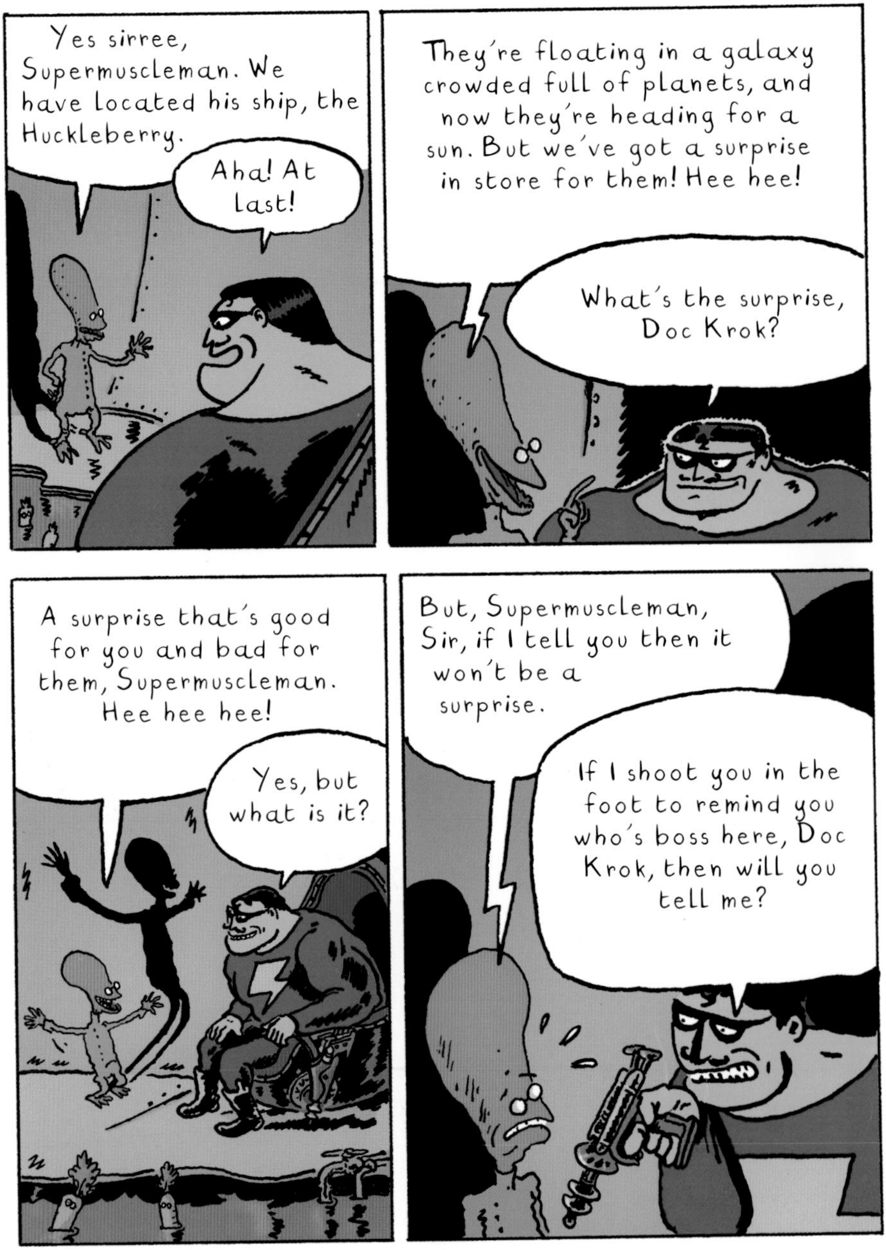
Yes sirree, Supermuscleman. We have located his ship, the Huckleberry.
Aha! At last!
They're floating in a galaxy crowded full of planets, and now they're heading for a sun. But we've got a surprise in store for them! Hee hee!
What's the surprise, Doc Krok?
A surprise that's good for you and bad for them, Supermuscleman. Hee hee hee!
Yes, but what is it?
But, Supermuscleman, Sir, if I tell you then it won't be a surprise.
If I shoot you in the foot to remind you who's boss here, Doc Krok, then will you tell me?

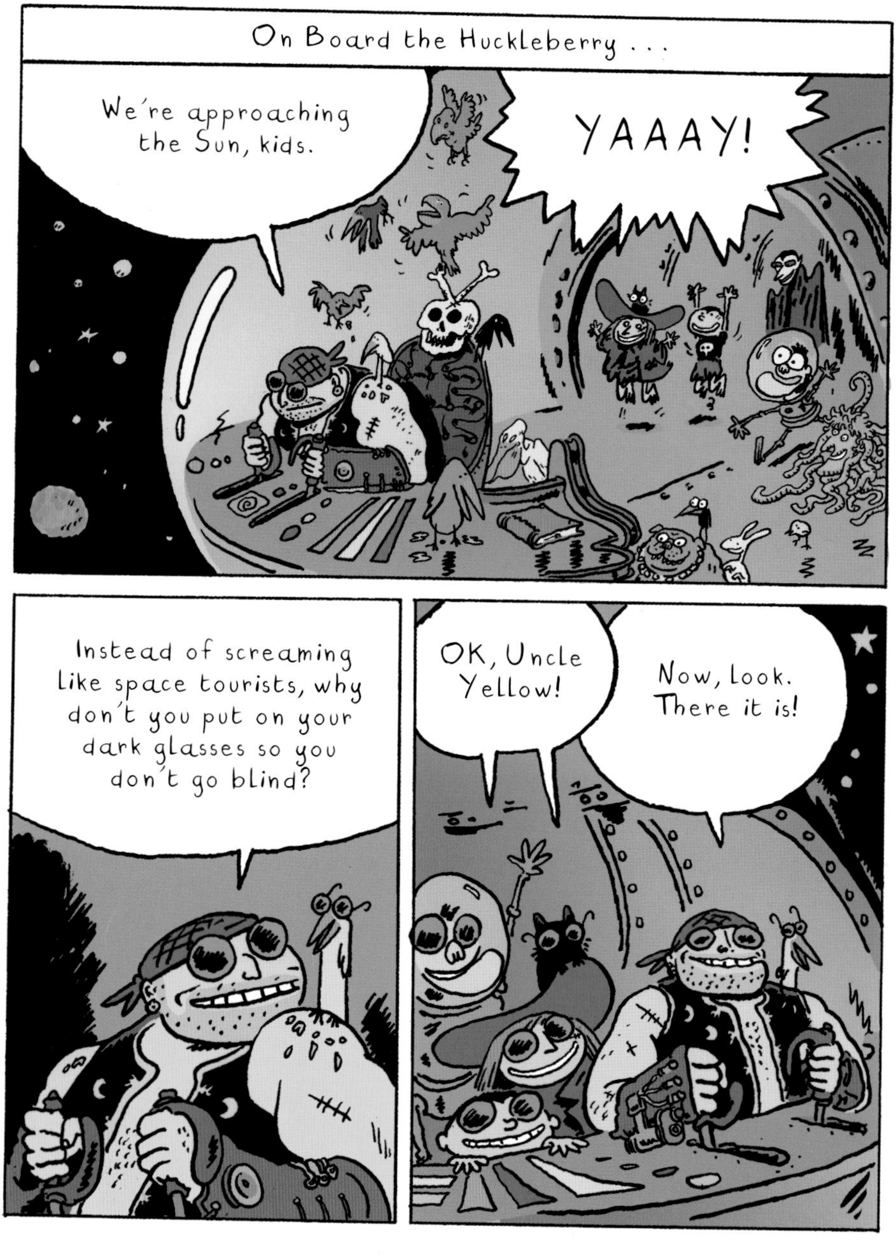

On Board the Huckleberry . . .
We're approaching the Sun, kids.
YAAAY!
Instead of screaming like space tourists, why don't you put on your dark glasses so you don't go blind?
OK, Uncle Yellow!
Now, look. There it is!

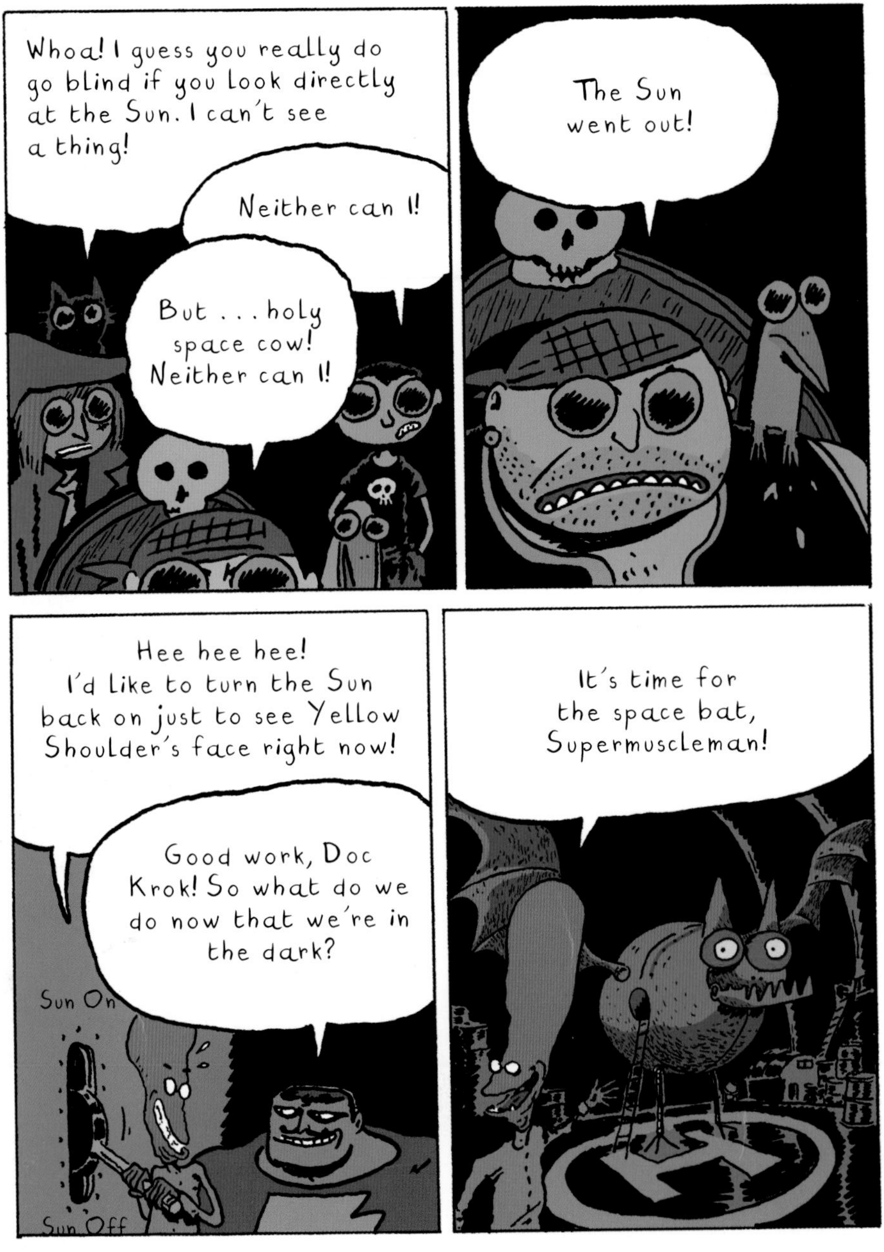
Whoa! I guess you really do go blind if you look directly at the Sun. I can't see a thing!
Neither can I!
But . . . holy space cow! Neither can I!
The Sun went out!
Hee hee hee! I'd like to turn the Sun back on just to see Yellow Shoulder's face right now!
Good work, Doc Krok! So what do we do now that we're in the dark?
Sun On
Sun Off
It's time for the space bat, Supermuscleman!

Go on, Supermuscleman!

Ouch! Don't push, Doc Krok!

Well, you shouldn't have shot yourself in the foot!

Shut up and let's go, you cheeky slug!

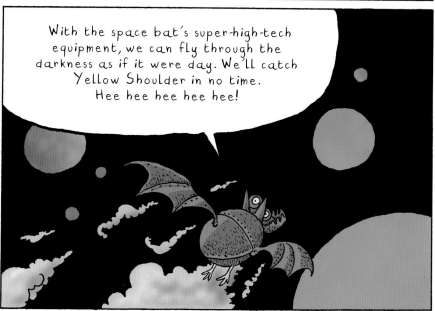

With the space bat's super-high-tech equipment, we can fly through the darkness as if it were day. We'll catch Yellow Shoulder in no time. Hee hee hee hee hee!

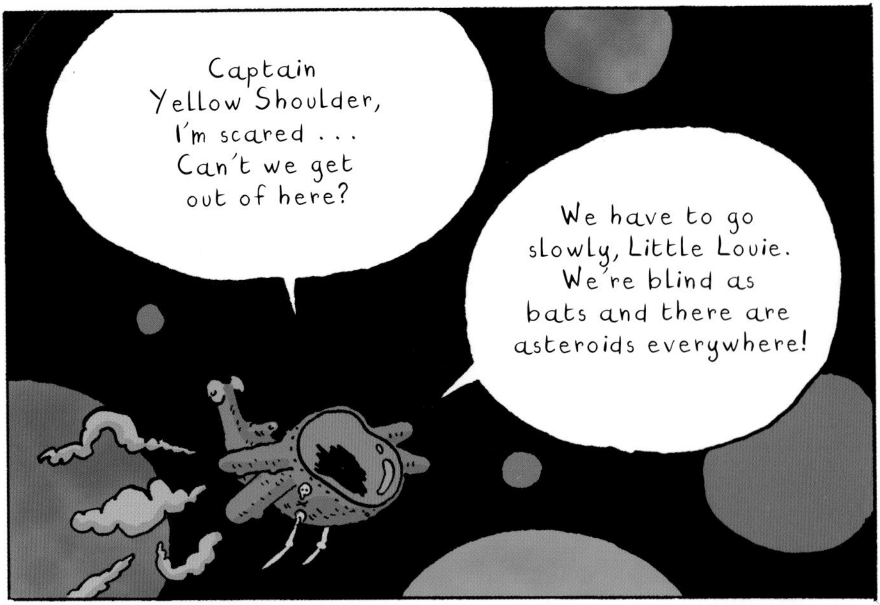
Captain Yellow Shoulder, I'm scared . . . Can't we get out of here?
We have to go slowly, Little Louie. We're blind as bats and there are asteroids everywhere!

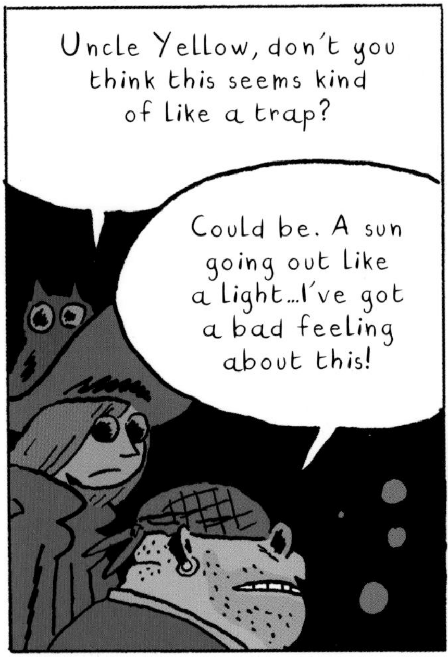
Uncle Yellow, don't you think this seems kind of like a trap?
Could be. A sun going out like a light...I've got a bad feeling about this!

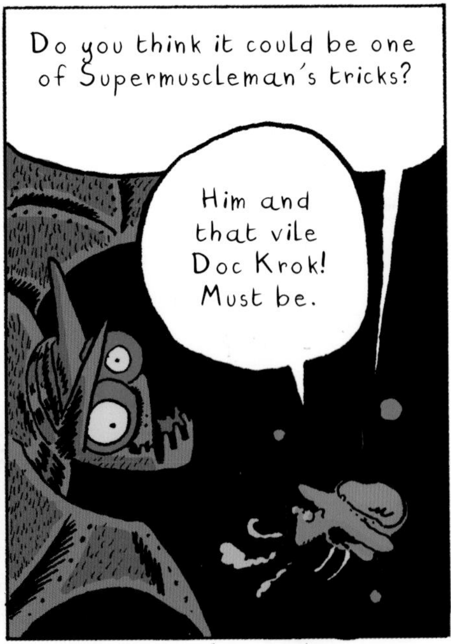
Do you think it could be one of Supermuscleman's tricks?
Him and that vile Doc Krok! Must be.

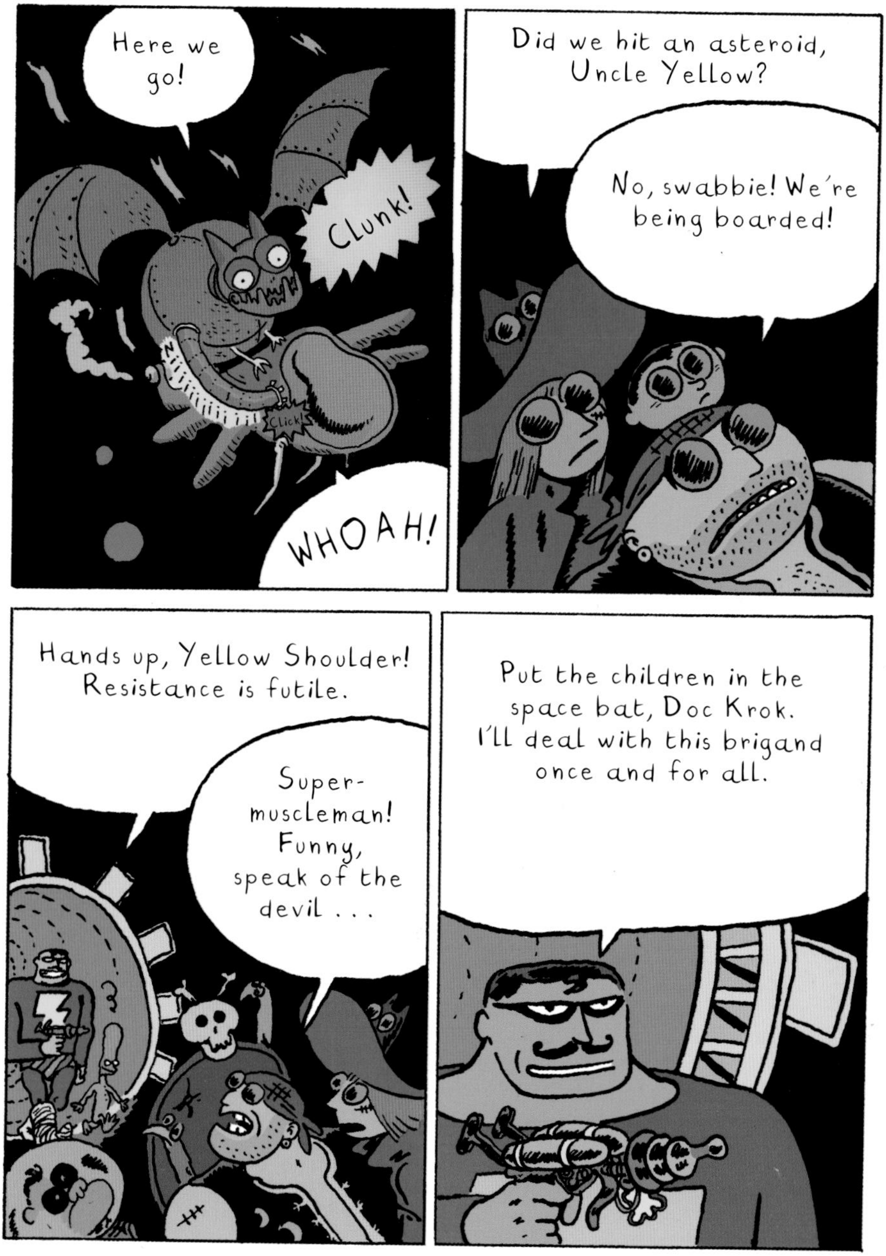
Here we go!
Clunk!
Click!
WHOAH!
Did we hit an asteroid, Uncle Yellow?
No, swabbie! We're being boarded!
Hands up, Yellow Shoulder! Resistance is futile.
Super-muscleman! Funny, speak of the devil . . .
Put the children in the space bat, Doc Krok. I'll deal with this brigand once and for all.

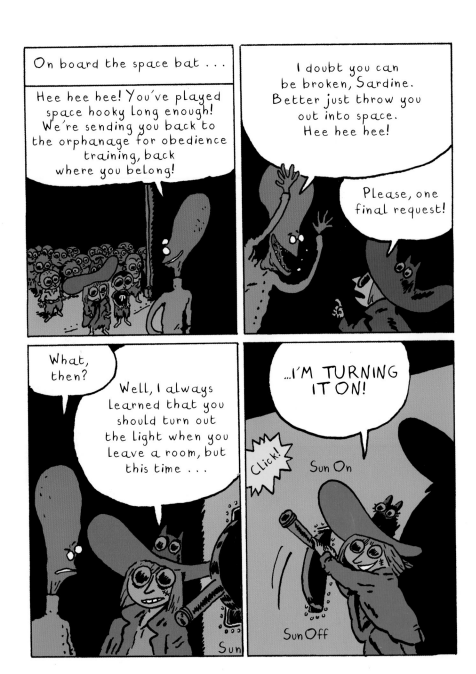

On board the space bat . . .

Hee hee hee! You've played space hooky long enough! We're sending you back to the orphanage for obedience training, back where you belong!

I doubt you can be broken, Sardine. Better just throw you out into space. Hee hee hee!

Please, one final request!

What, then?

Well, I always learned that you should turn out the light when you leave a room, but this time . . .

Sun

...I'M TURNING IT ON!

Click!

Sun On

Sun Off

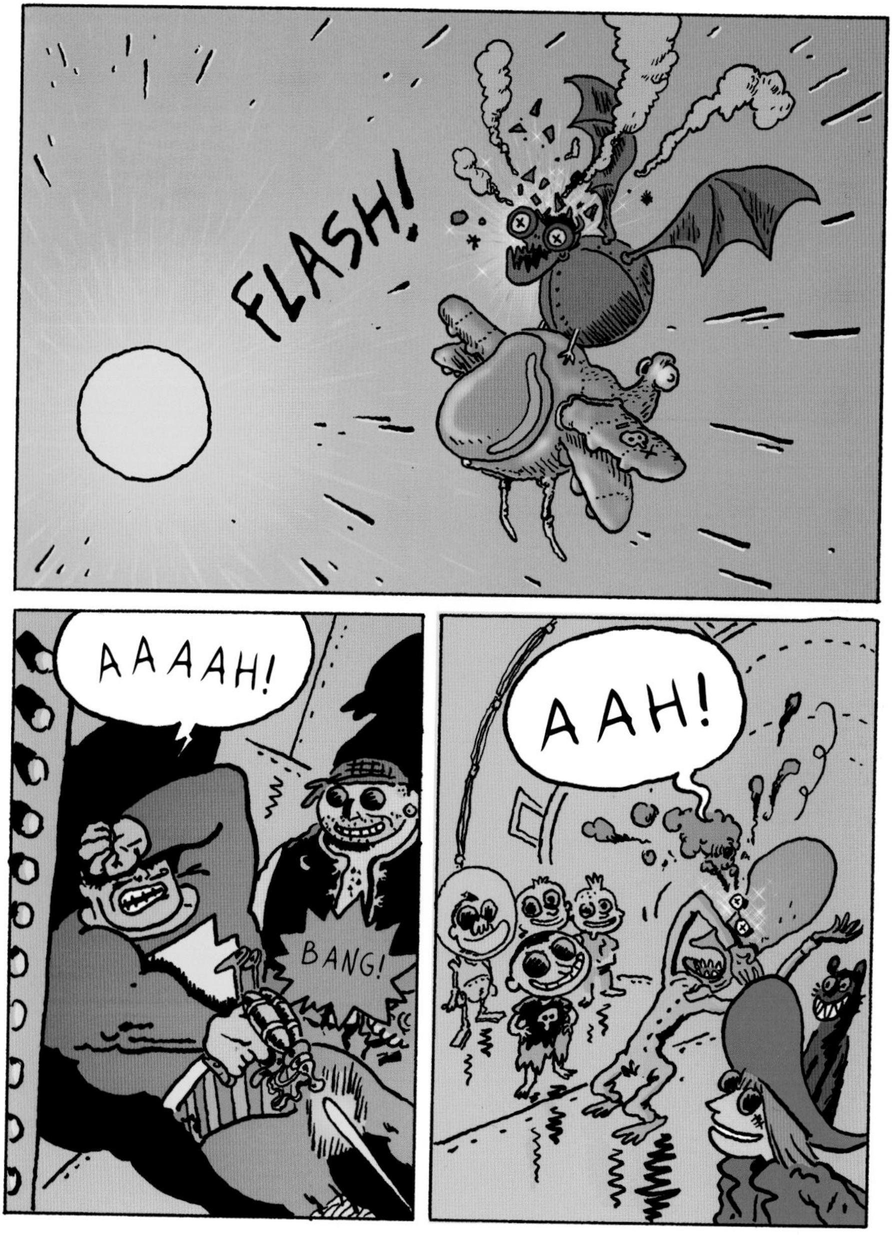
FLASH!
AAAAH!
BANG!
AAH!

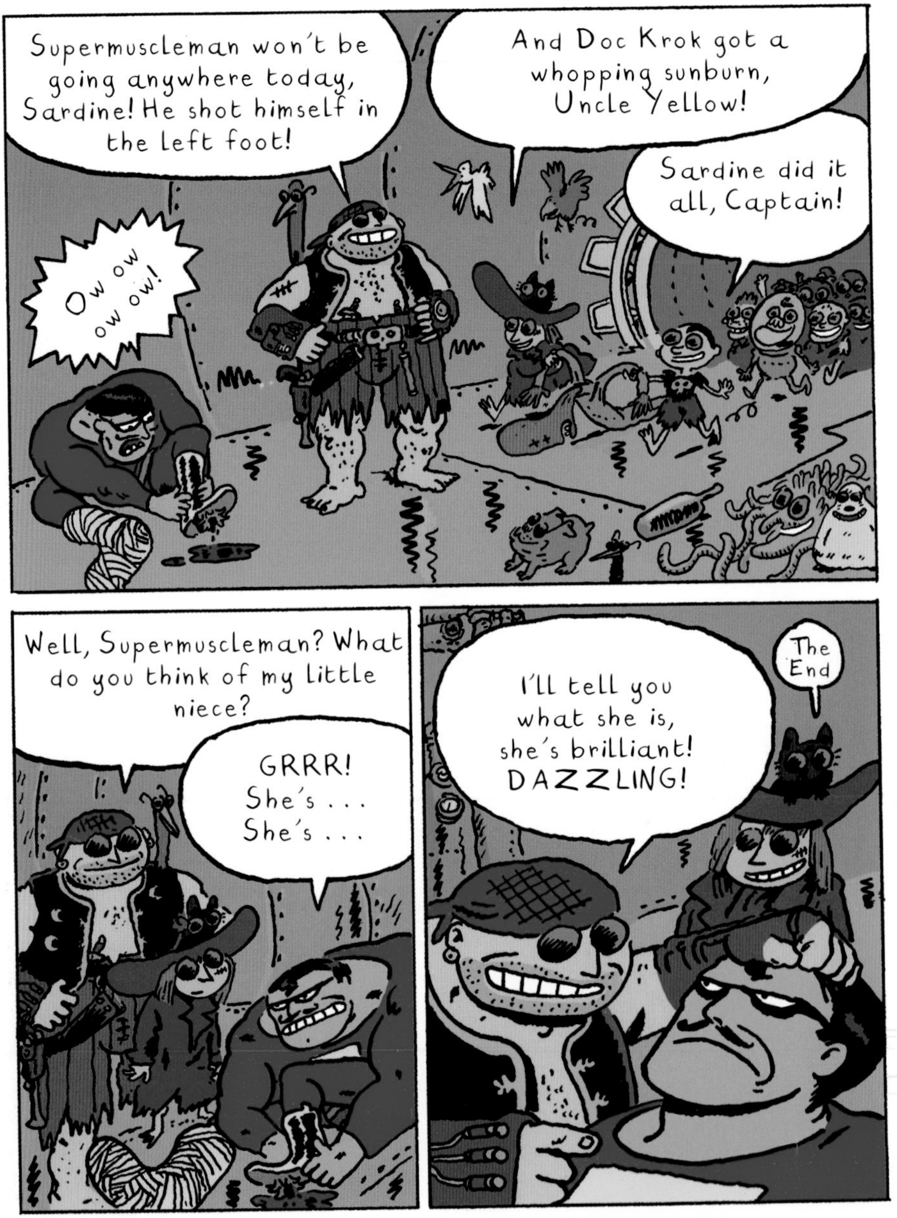
Supermuscleman won't be going anywhere today, Sardine! He shot himself in the left foot!
And Doc Krok got a whopping sunburn, Uncle Yellow!
Sardine did it all, Captain!
Ow ow ow ow!
Well, Supermuscleman? What do you think of my little niece?
GRRR! She's . . . She's . . .
I'll tell you what she is, she's brilliant! DAZZLING!
The End

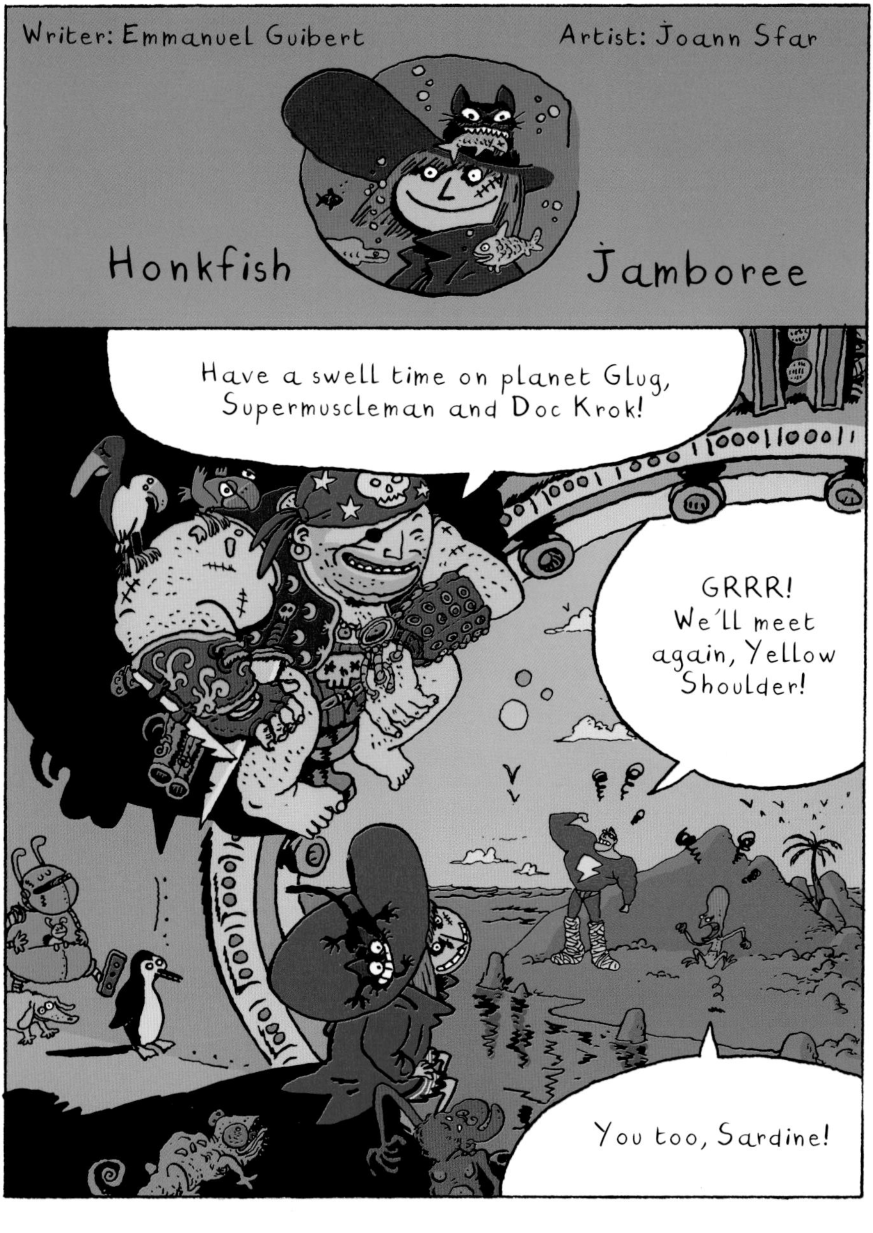
Writer: Emmanuel Guibert
Artist: Joann Sfar
Honkfish Jamboree
Have a swell time on planet Glug, Supermuscleman and Doc Krok!
GRRR! We'll meet again, Yellow Shoulder!
You too, Sardine!

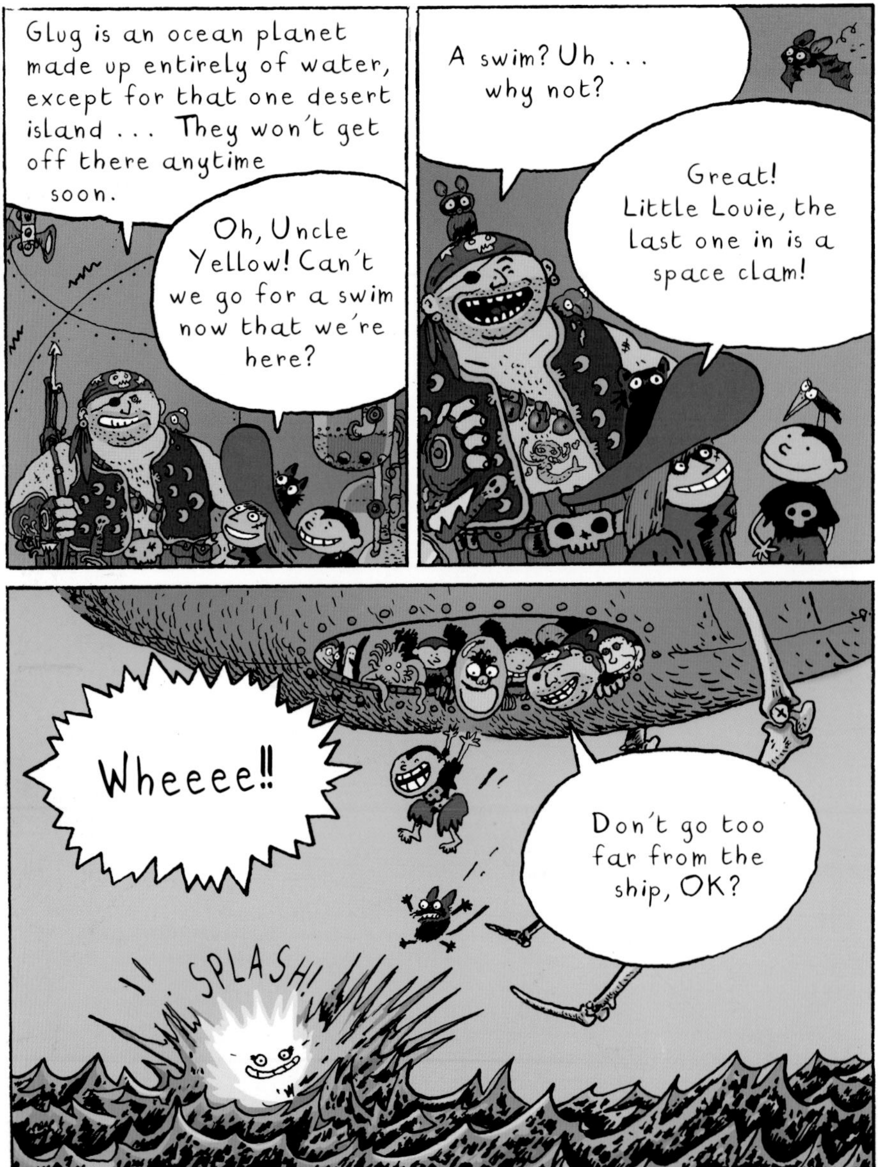
Glug is an ocean planet made up entirely of water, except for that one desert island . . . They won't get off there anytime soon.
Oh, Uncle Yellow! Can't we go for a swim now that we're here?
A swim? Uh . . . why not?
Great! Little Louie, the last one in is a space clam!
Wheeee!!
Don't go too far from the ship, OK?
SPLASH!

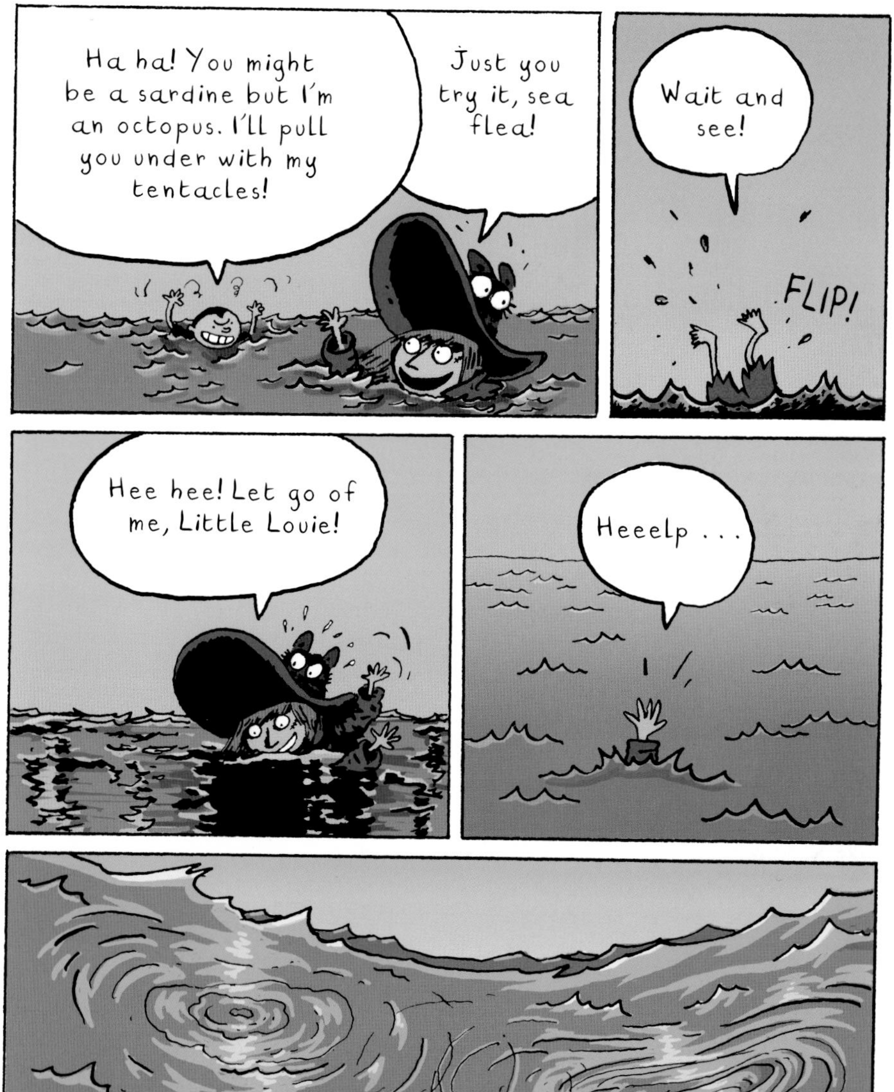
Ha ha! You might be a sardine but I'm an octopus. I'll pull you under with my tentacles!
Just you try it, sea flea!
Wait and see!
FLIP!
Hee hee! Let go of me, Little Louie!
Heeelp . . .

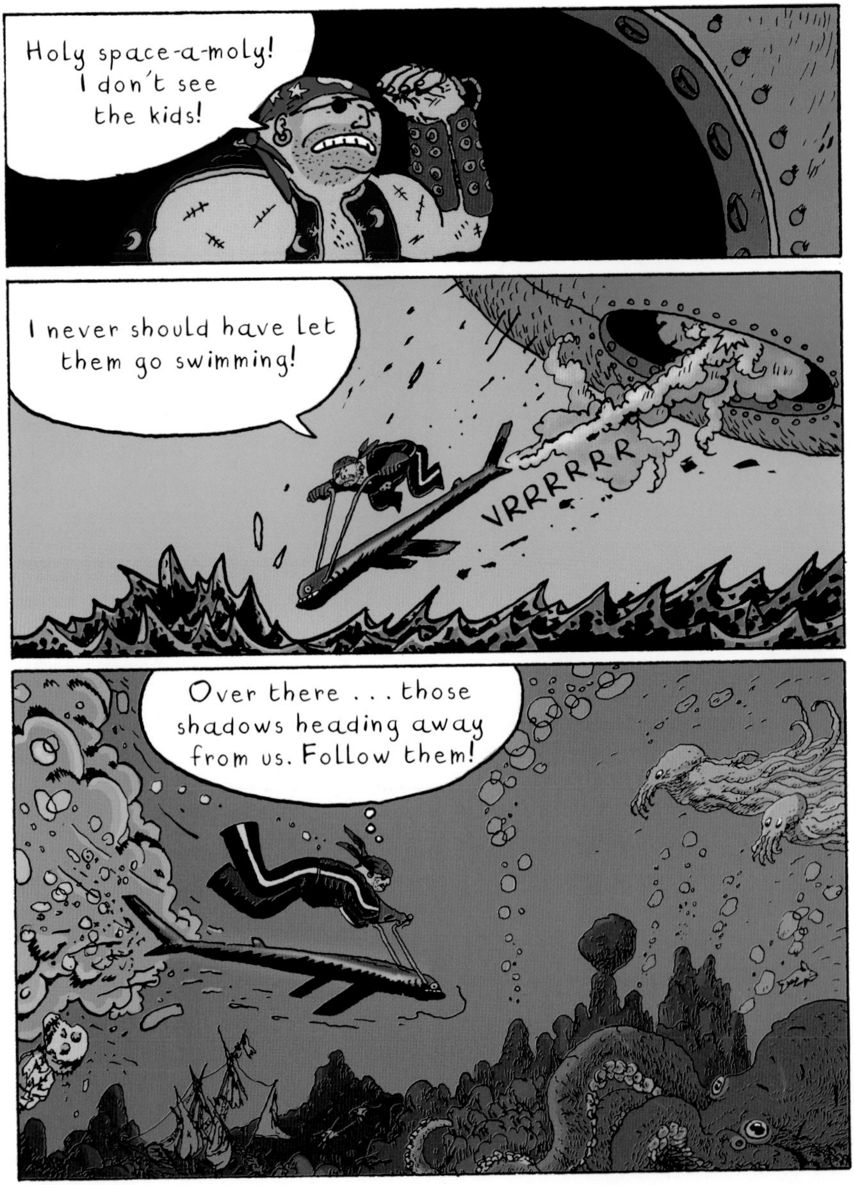
Holy space-a-moly! I don't see the kids!
I never should have let them go swimming!
VRRRRRR
Over there . . . those shadows heading away from us. Follow them!

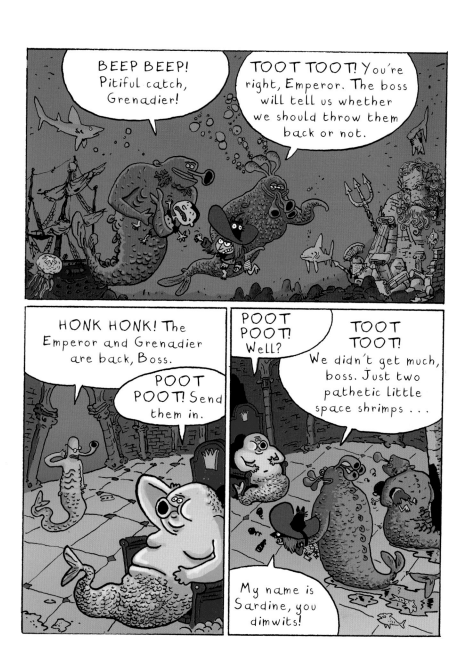

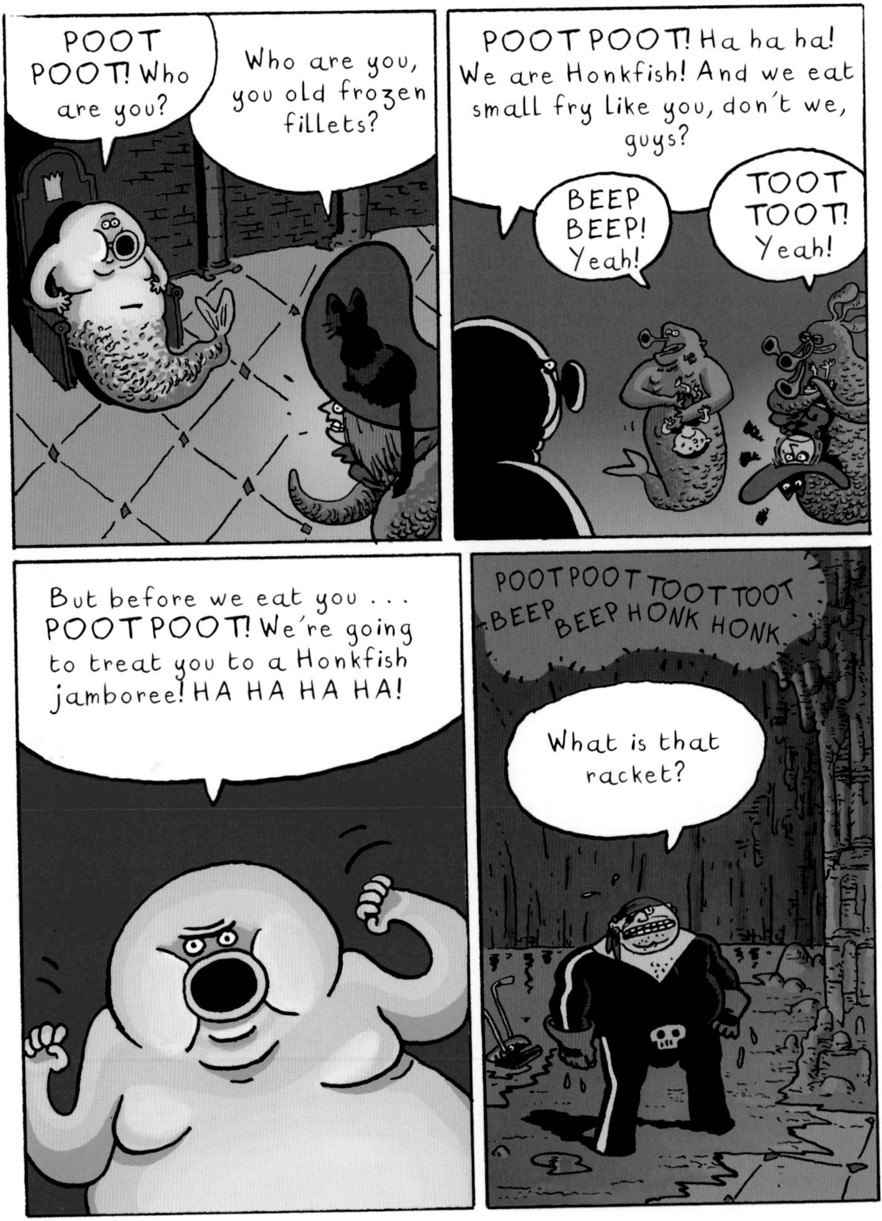
POOT POOT! Who are you?
Who are you, you old frozen fillets?
POOT POOT! Ha ha ha! We are Honkfish! And we eat small fry like you, don't we, guys?
BEEP BEEP! Yeah!
TOOT TOOT! Yeah!
But before we eat you . . . POOT POOT! We're going to treat you to a Honkfish jamboree! HA HA HA HA!
POOT POOT TOOT TOOT BEEP BEEP HONK HONK
What is that racket?

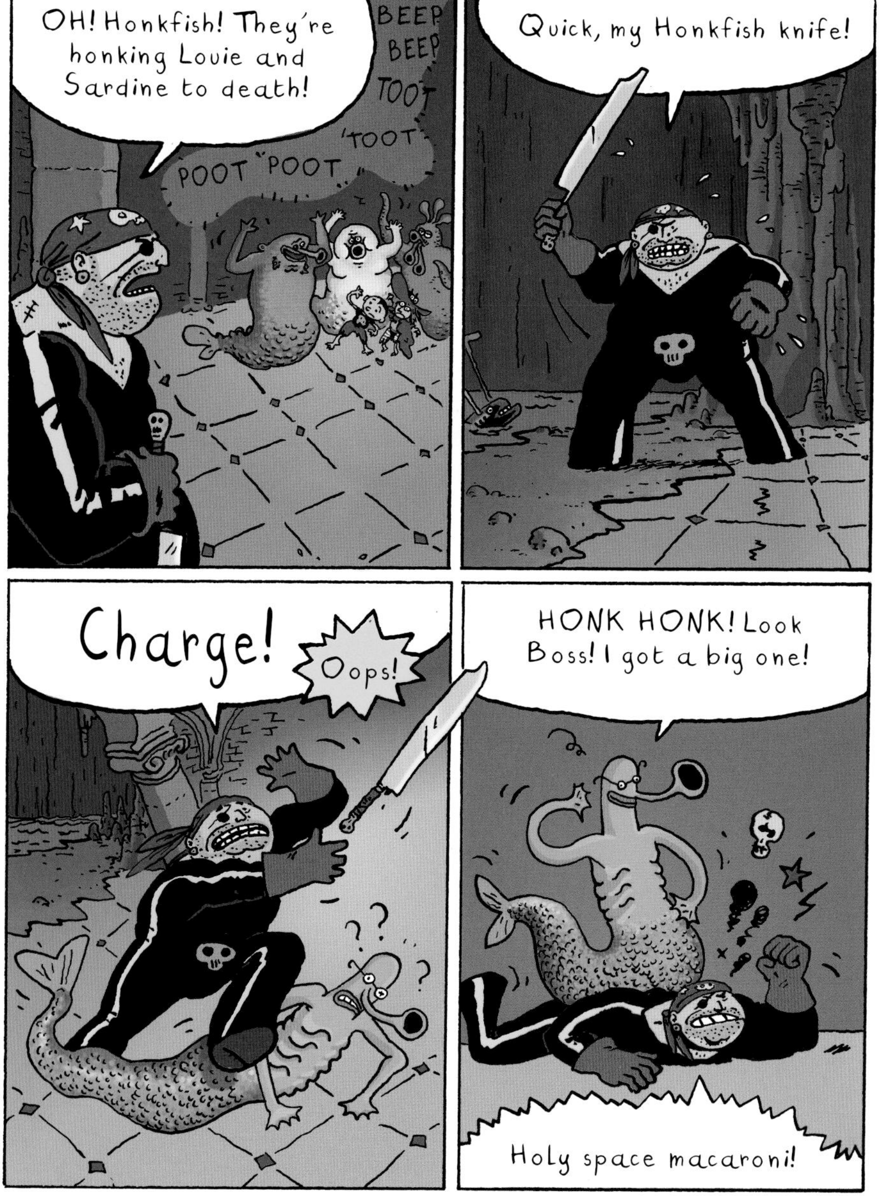
OH! Honkfish! They're honking Louie and Sardine to death!
BEEP BEEP TOOT TOOT POOT POOT
Quick, my Honkfish knife!
Charge!
Oops!
HONK HONK! Look Boss! I got a big one!
Holy space macaroni!

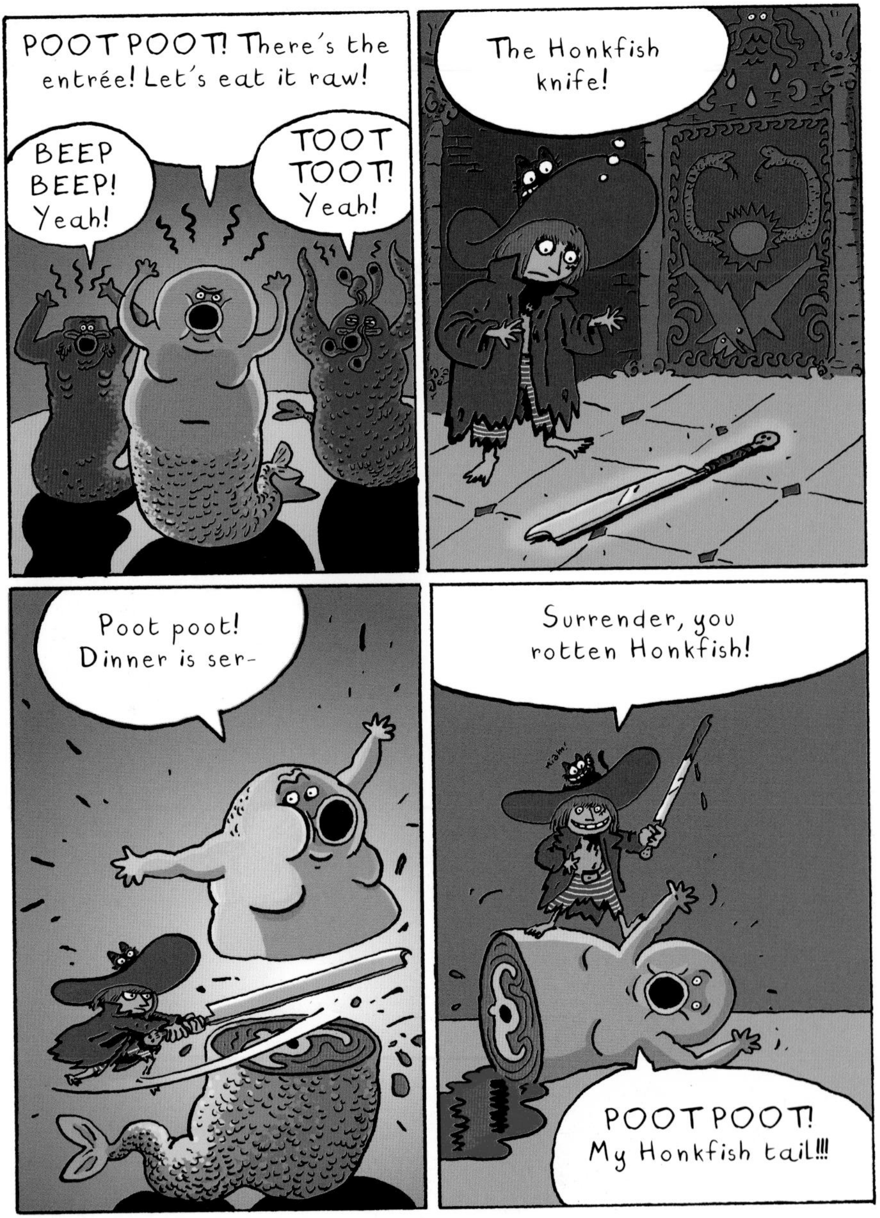
POOTPOOT! There's the entrée! Let's eat it raw!
BEEP BEEP! Yeah!
TOOT TOOT! Yeah!
The Honkfish knife!
Poot poot! Dinner is ser-
Surrender, you rotten Honkfish!
POOTPOOT! My Honkfish tail!!!

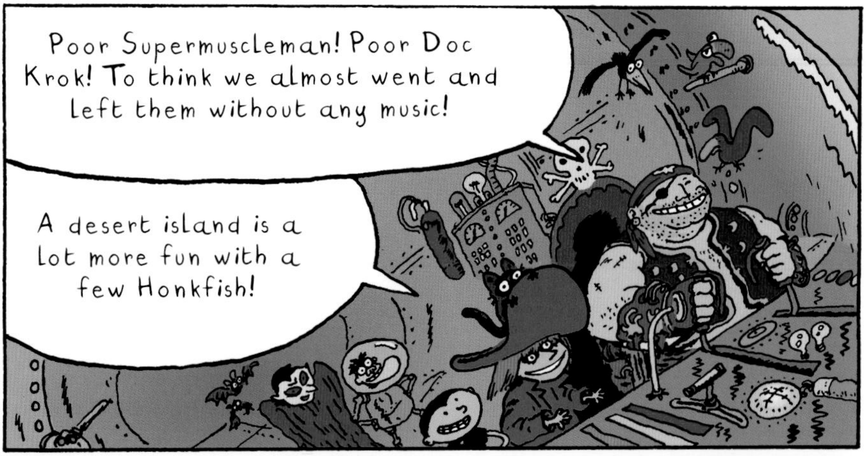
Poor Supermuscleman! Poor Doc Krok! To think we almost went and left them without any music!
A desert island is a lot more fun with a few Honkfish!

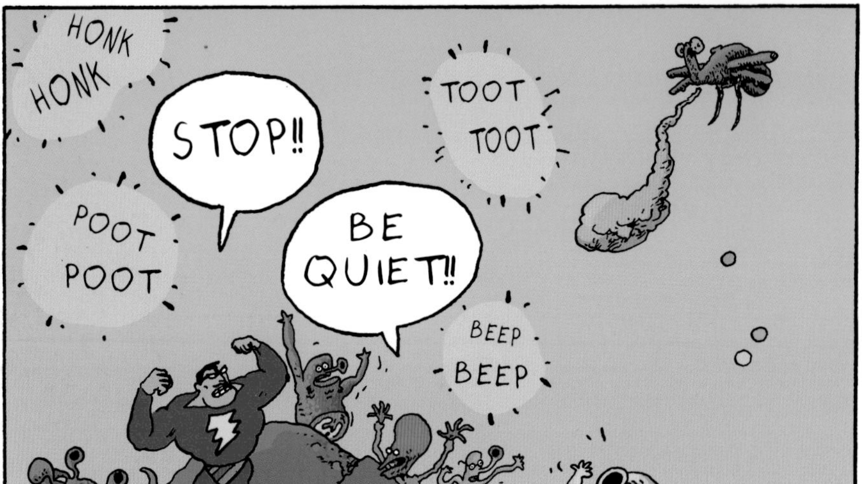
HONK HONK
STOP!!
TOOT TOOT
POOT POOT
BE QUIET!!
BEEP BEEP
The End

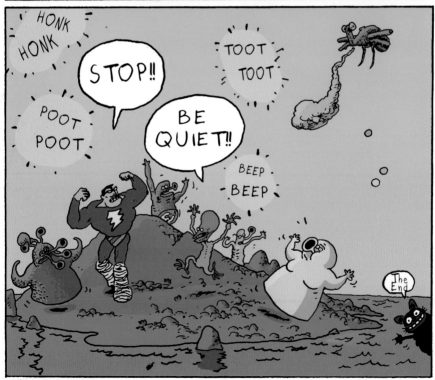

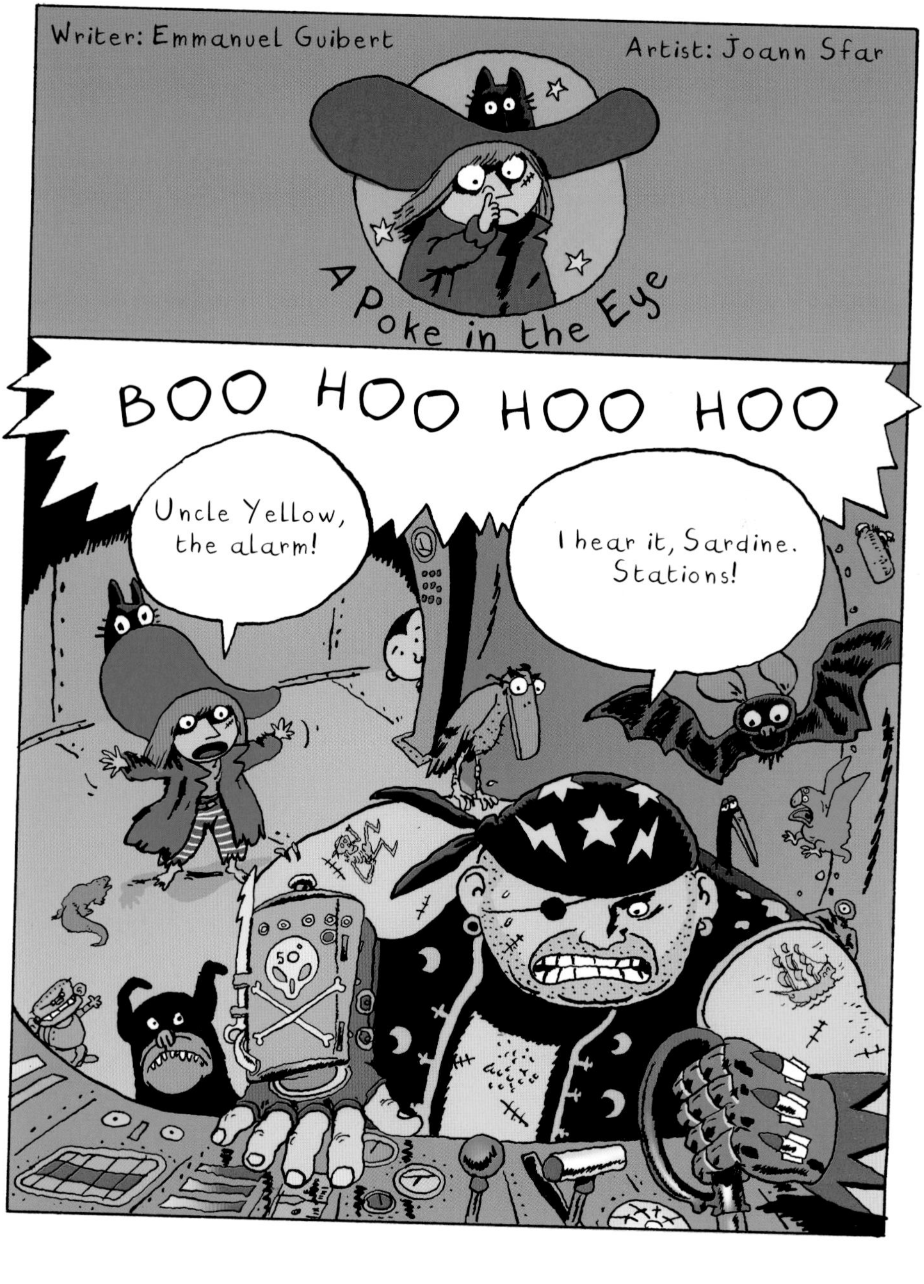
Writer: Emmanuel Guibert
Artist: Joann Sfar
A Poke in the Eye
BOO HOO HOO HOO
Uncle Yellow, the alarm!
I hear it, Sardine. Stations!
50

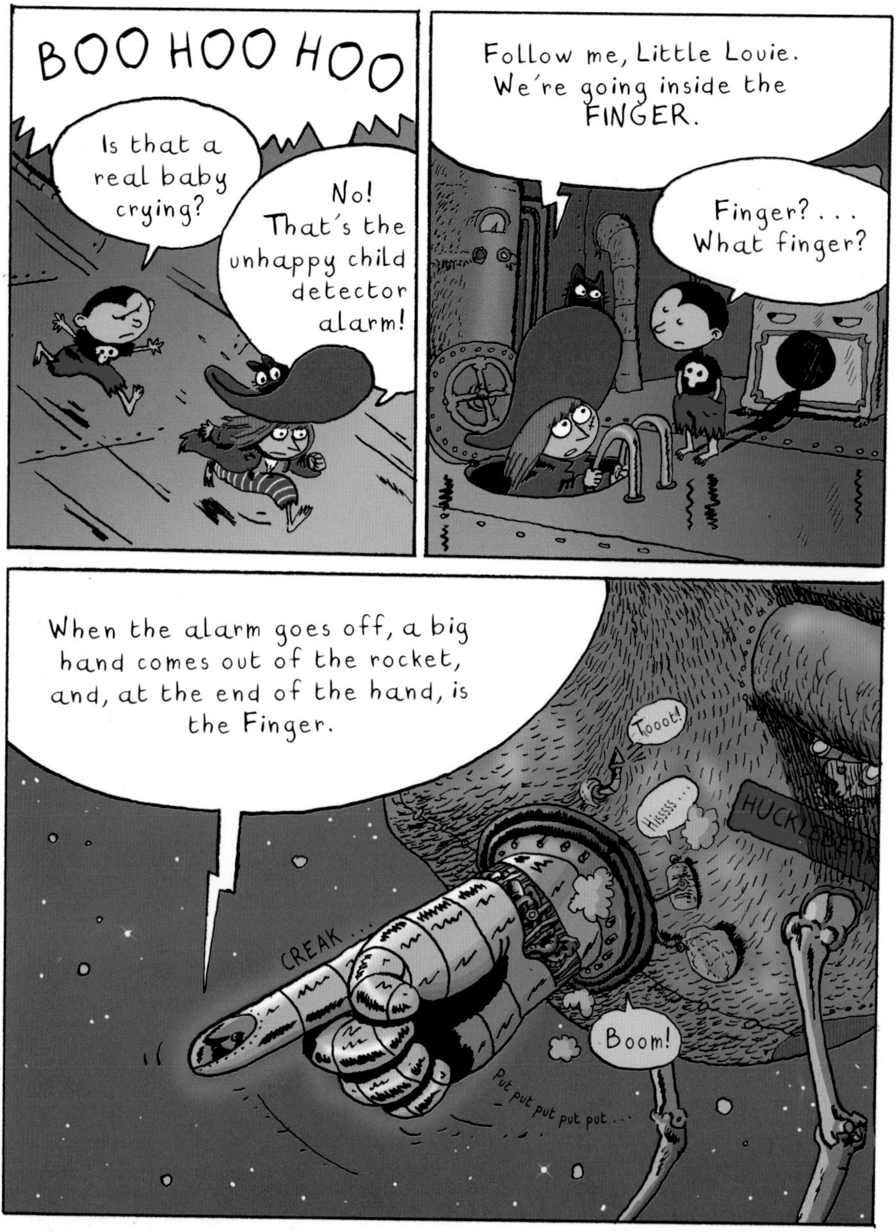
BOO HOO HOO
Is that a real baby crying?
No! That's the unhappy child detector alarm!
Follow me, Little Louie. We're going inside the FINGER.
Finger? . . . What finger?
When the alarm goes off, a big hand comes out of the rocket, and, at the end of the hand, is the Finger.
Tooot!
Hissss . . .
CREAK . . .
Boom!
Put put put put put . . .

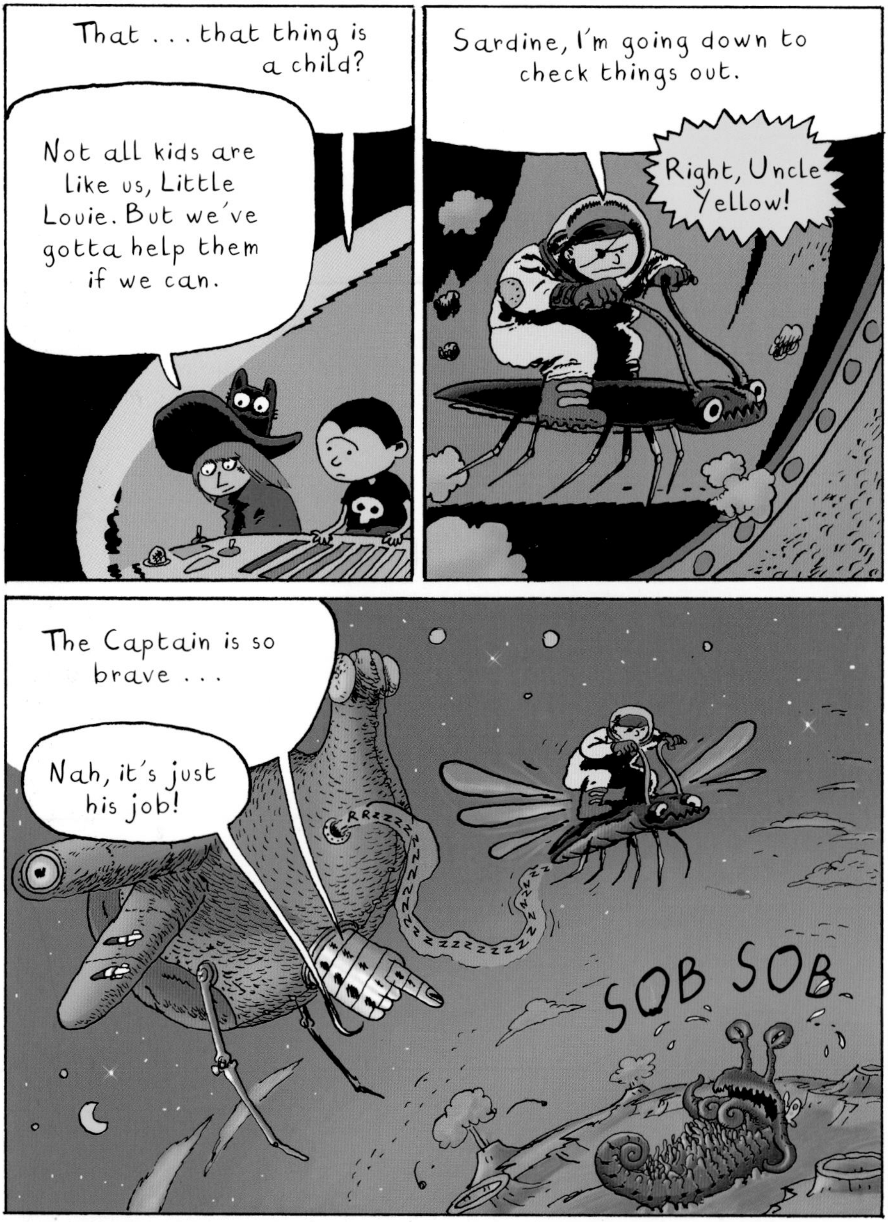
That . . . that thing is a child?
Not all kids are like us, Little Louie. But we've gotta help them if we can.
Sardine, I'm going down to check things out.
Right, Uncle Yellow!
The Captain is so brave . . .
Nah, it's just his job!
RRzzzz
SOB SOB

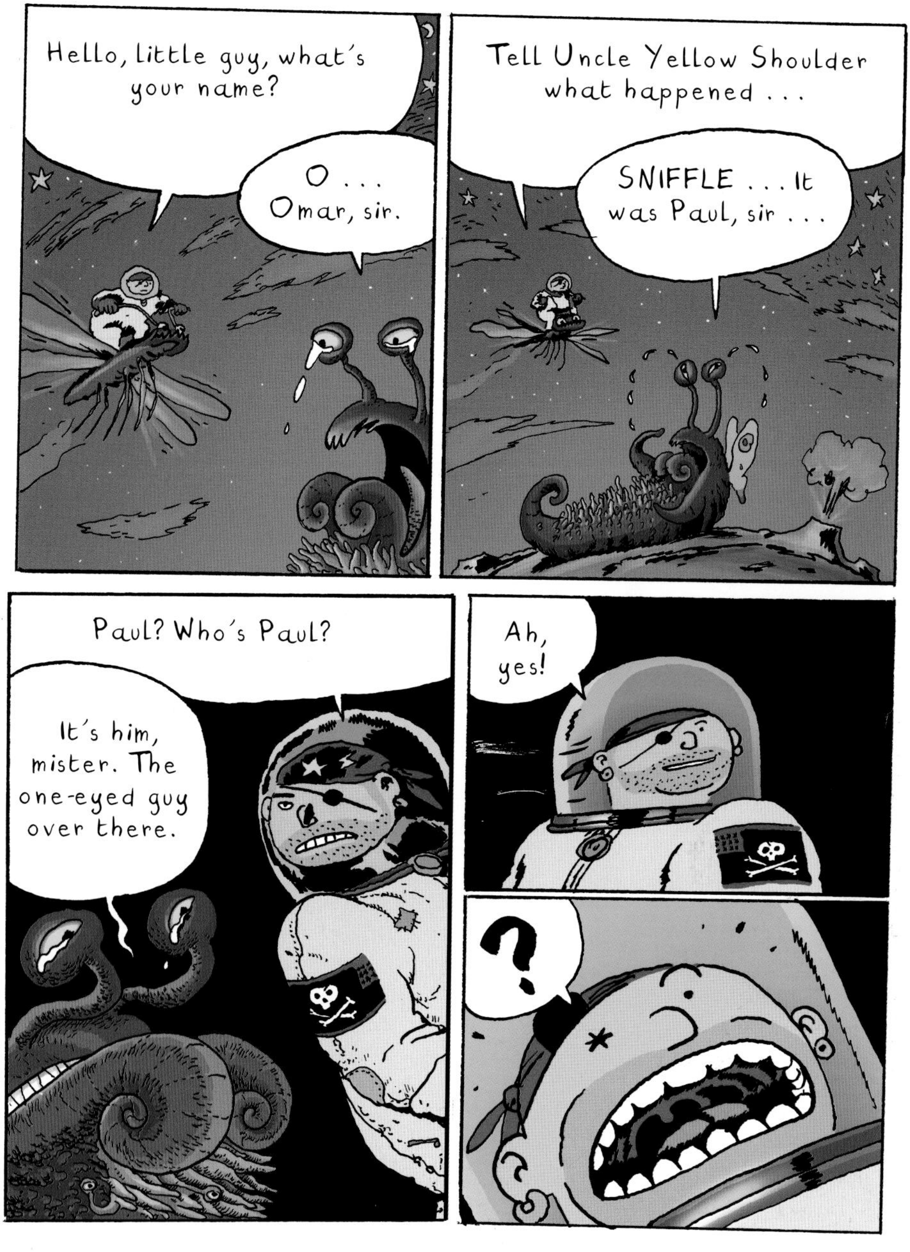
Hello, little guy, what's your name?
O . . . Omar, sir.
Tell Uncle Yellow Shoulder what happened . . .
SNIFFLE . . . It was Paul, sir . . .
Paul? Who's Paul?
It's him, mister. The one-eyed guy over there.
Ah, yes!
?

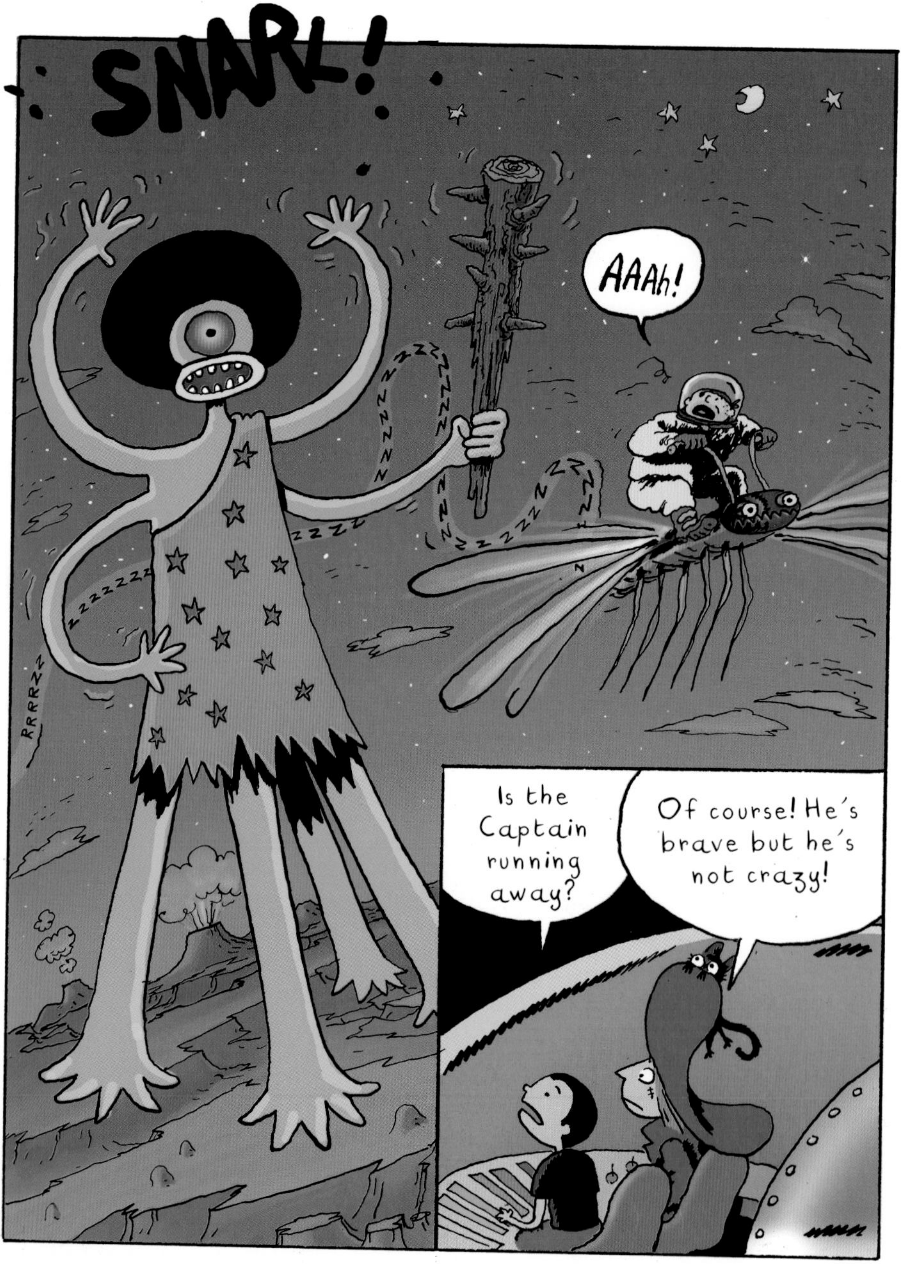
SNARL!
AAAh!
Is the Captain running away?
Of course! He's brave but he's not crazy!

When you said we were going to have bad manners, I thought you wanted to put the finger in his nose!

Eeeeew! Gross!

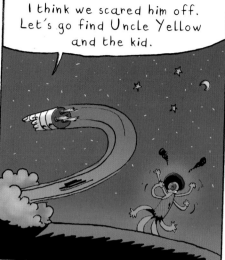

I think we scared him off. Let's go find Uncle Yellow and the kid.

Omar, that nasty Paul won't be bothering you anymore. Do you want to stay here or come travel through outer space with me and my crew?

Oh, I'm all right here. This is my home.

SPLAATT!

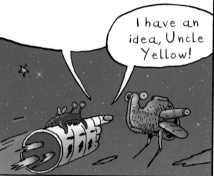

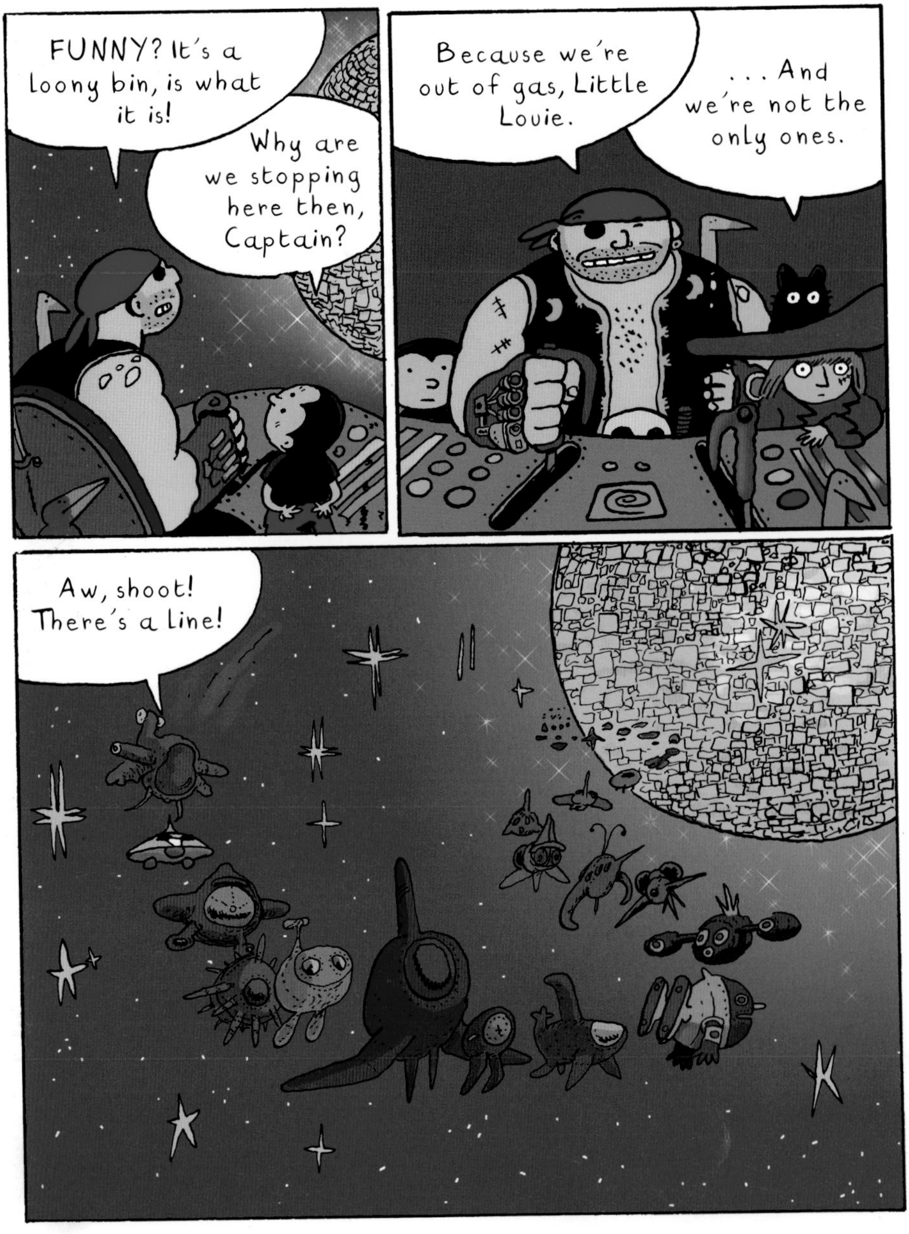
FUNNY? It's a loony bin, is what it is!
Why are we stopping here then, Captain?
Because we're out of gas, Little Louie.
. . . And we're not the only ones.
Aw, shoot! There's a line!

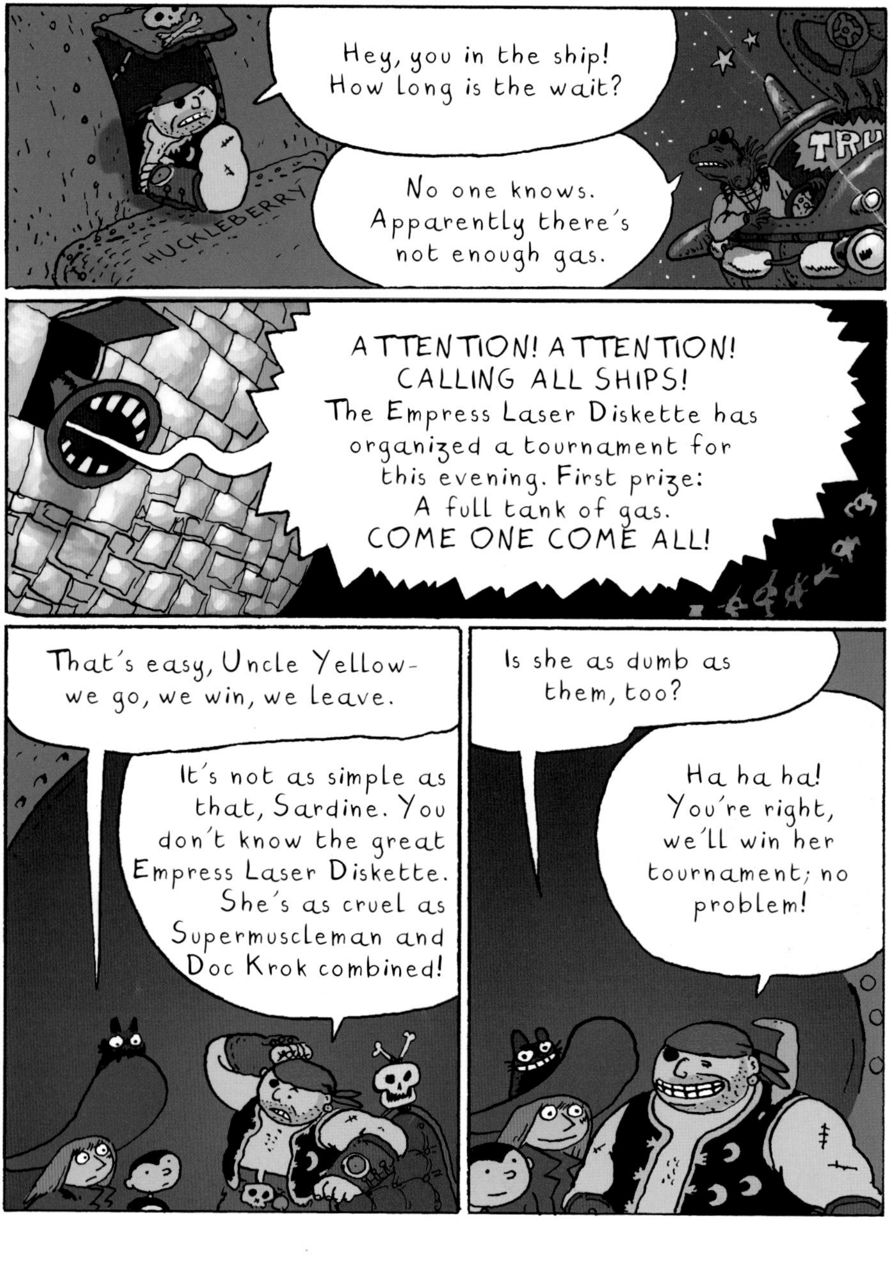

Hey, you in the ship! How long is the wait?
HUCKLEBERRY
No one knows. Apparently there's not enough gas.
TRU
ATTENTION! ATTENTION! CALLING ALL SHIPS! The Empress Laser Diskette has organized a tournament for this evening. First prize: A full tank of gas. COME ONE COME ALL!
That's easy, Uncle Yellow- we go, we win, we leave.
It's not as simple as that, Sardine. You don't know the great Empress Laser Diskette. She's as cruel as Supermuscleman and Doc Krok combined!
Is she as dumb as them, too?
Ha ha ha! You're right, we'll win her tournament; no problem!

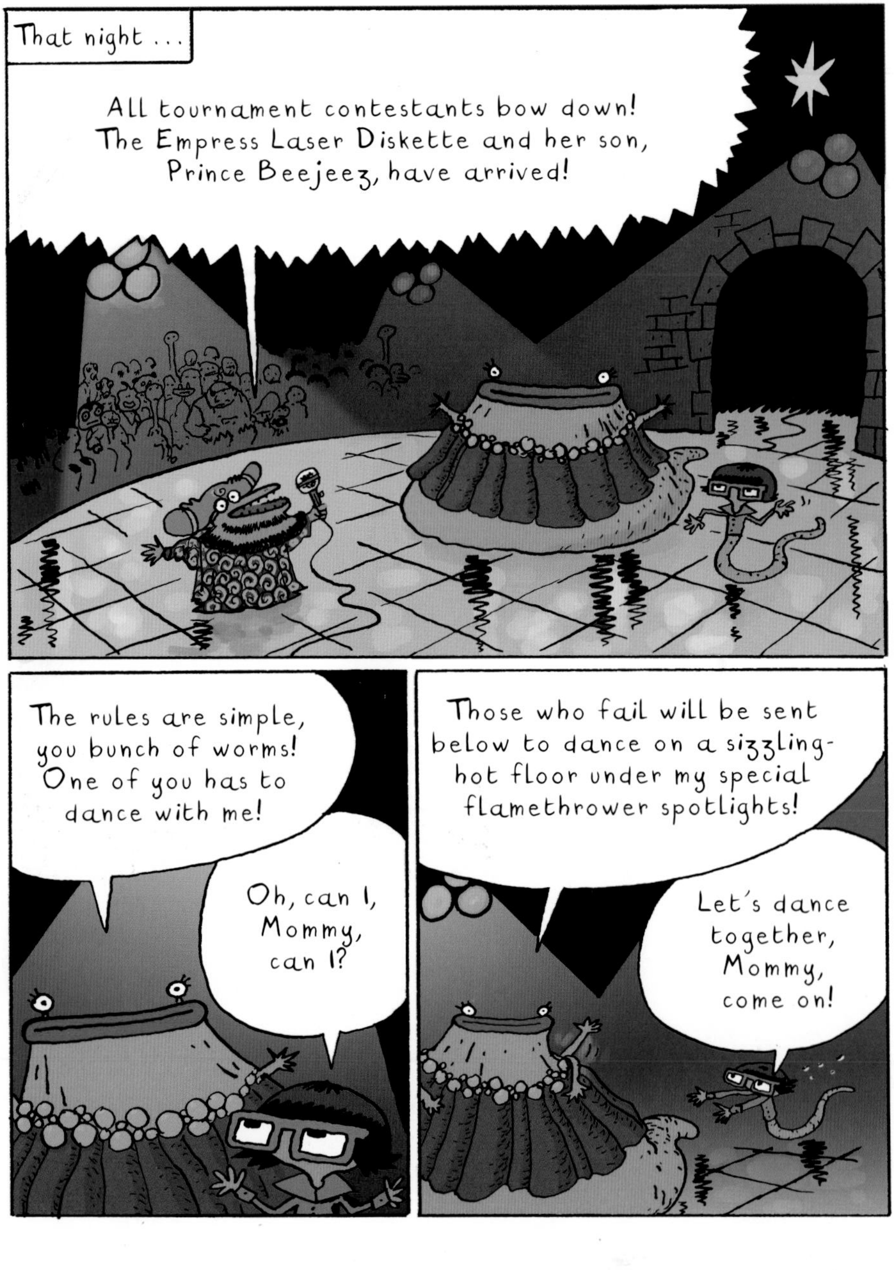

That night . . .
All tournament contestants bow down! The Empress Laser Diskette and her son, Prince Beejeez, have arrived!
The rules are simple, you bunch of worms! One of you has to dance with me!
Oh, can I, Mommy, can I?
Those who fail will be sent below to dance on a sizzling-hot floor under my special flamethrower spotlights!
Let's dance together, Mommy, come on!

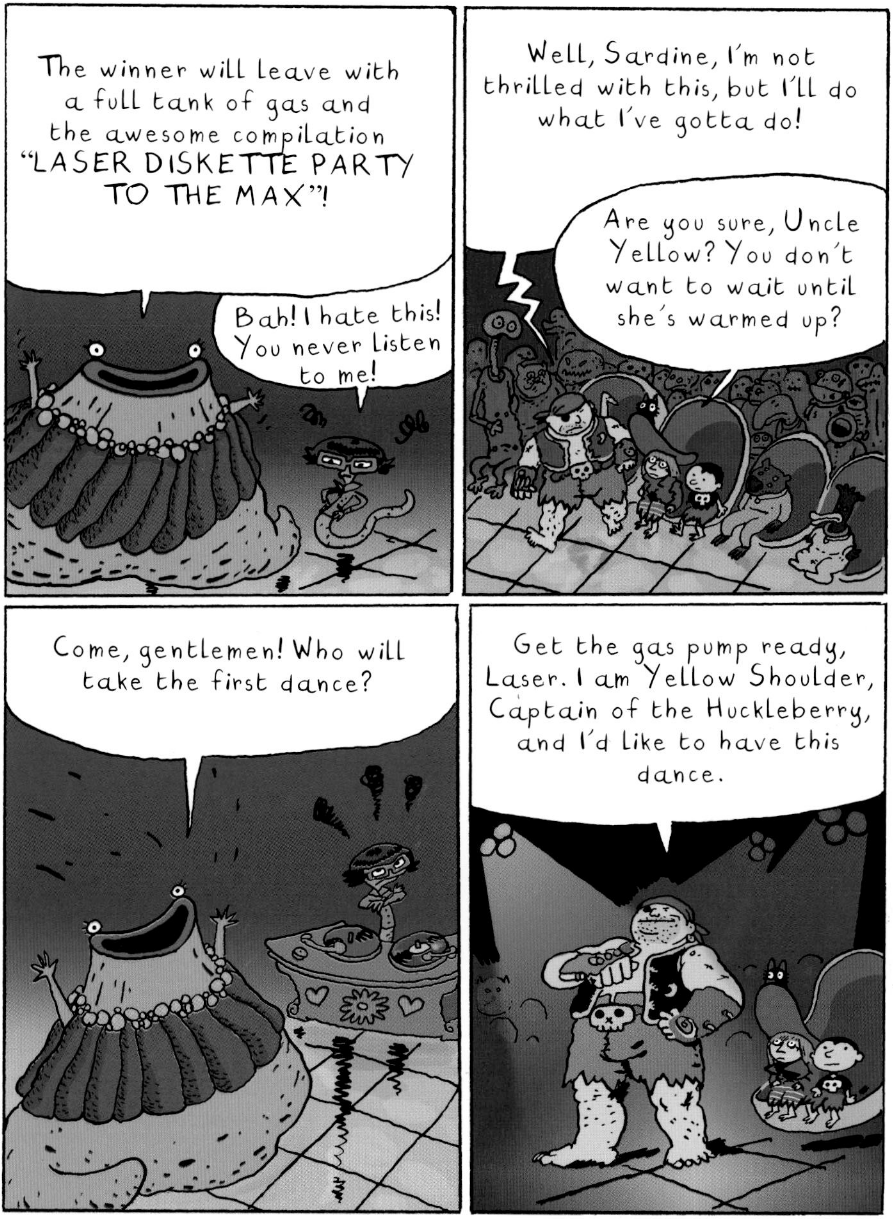

The winner will leave with a full tank of gas and the awesome compilation "LASER DISKETTE PARTY TO THE MAX"!
Bah! I hate this! You never listen to me!
Well, Sardine, I'm not thrilled with this, but I'll do what I've gotta do!
Are you sure, Uncle Yellow? You don't want to wait until she's warmed up?
Come, gentlemen! Who will take the first dance?
Get the gas pump ready, Laser. I am Yellow Shoulder, Captain of the Huckleberry, and I'd like to have this dance.

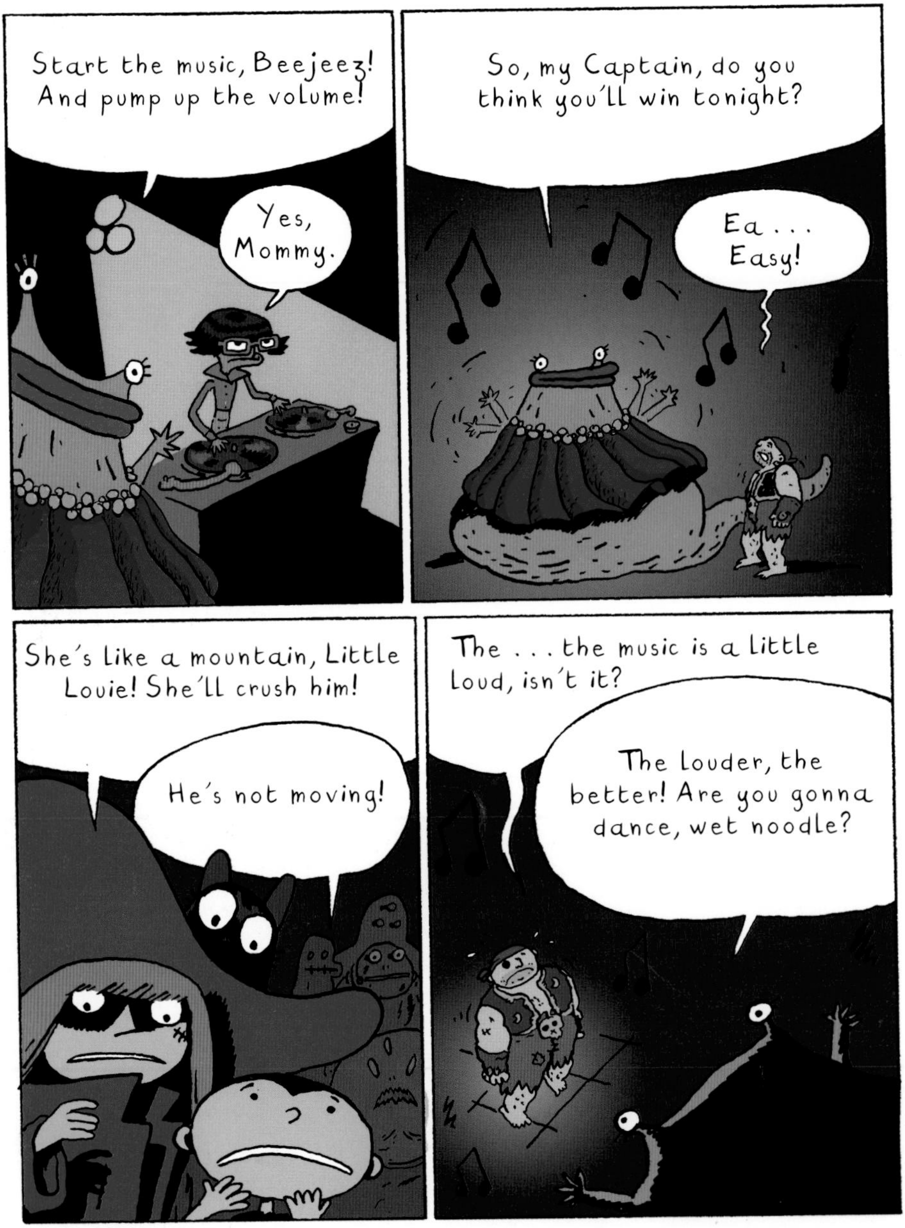
Start the music, Beejeez! And pump up the volume!
Yes, Mommy.
So, my Captain, do you think you'll win tonight?
Ea . . . Easy!
She's like a mountain, Little Louie! She'll crush him!
He's not moving!
The . . . the music is a little loud, isn't it?
The louder, the better! Are you gonna dance, wet noodle?

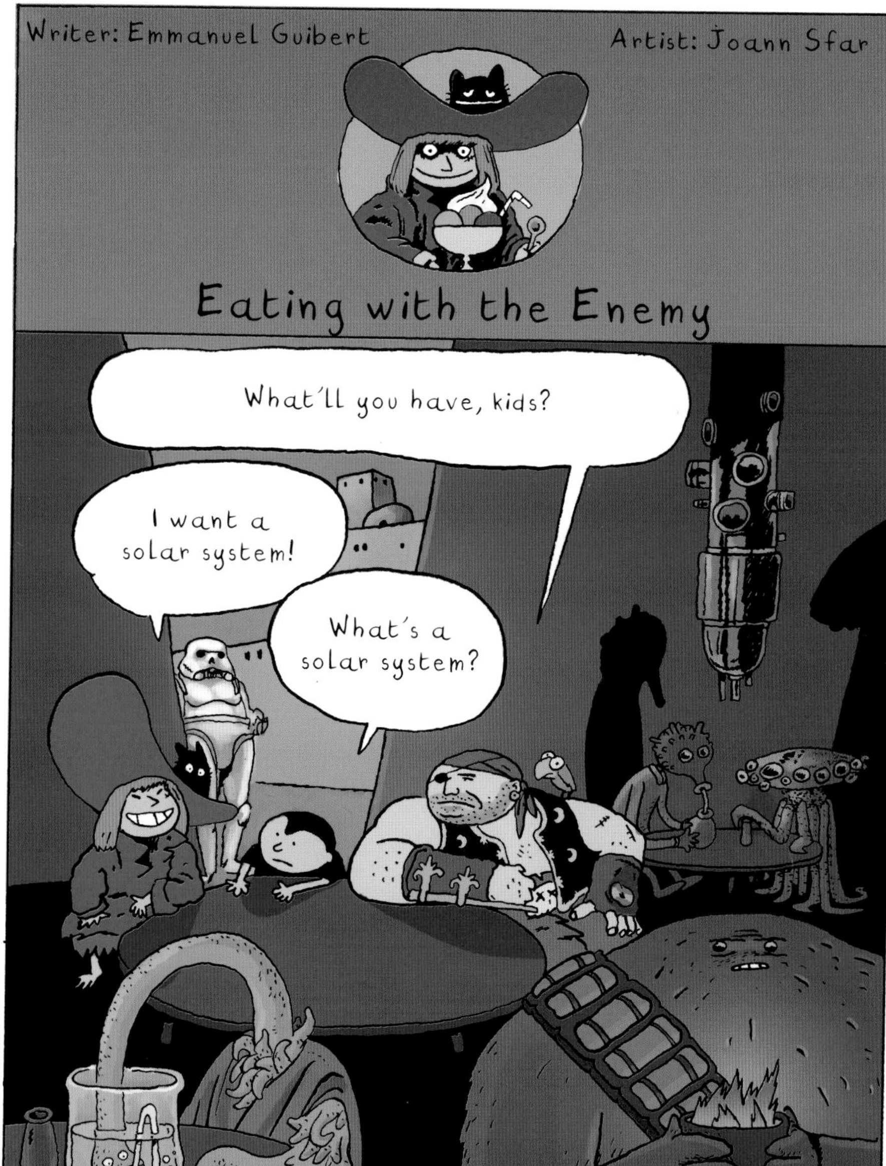
Writer: Emmanuel Guibert
Artist: Joann Sfar
Eating with the Enemy
What'll you have, kids?
I want a solar system!
What's a solar system?

65

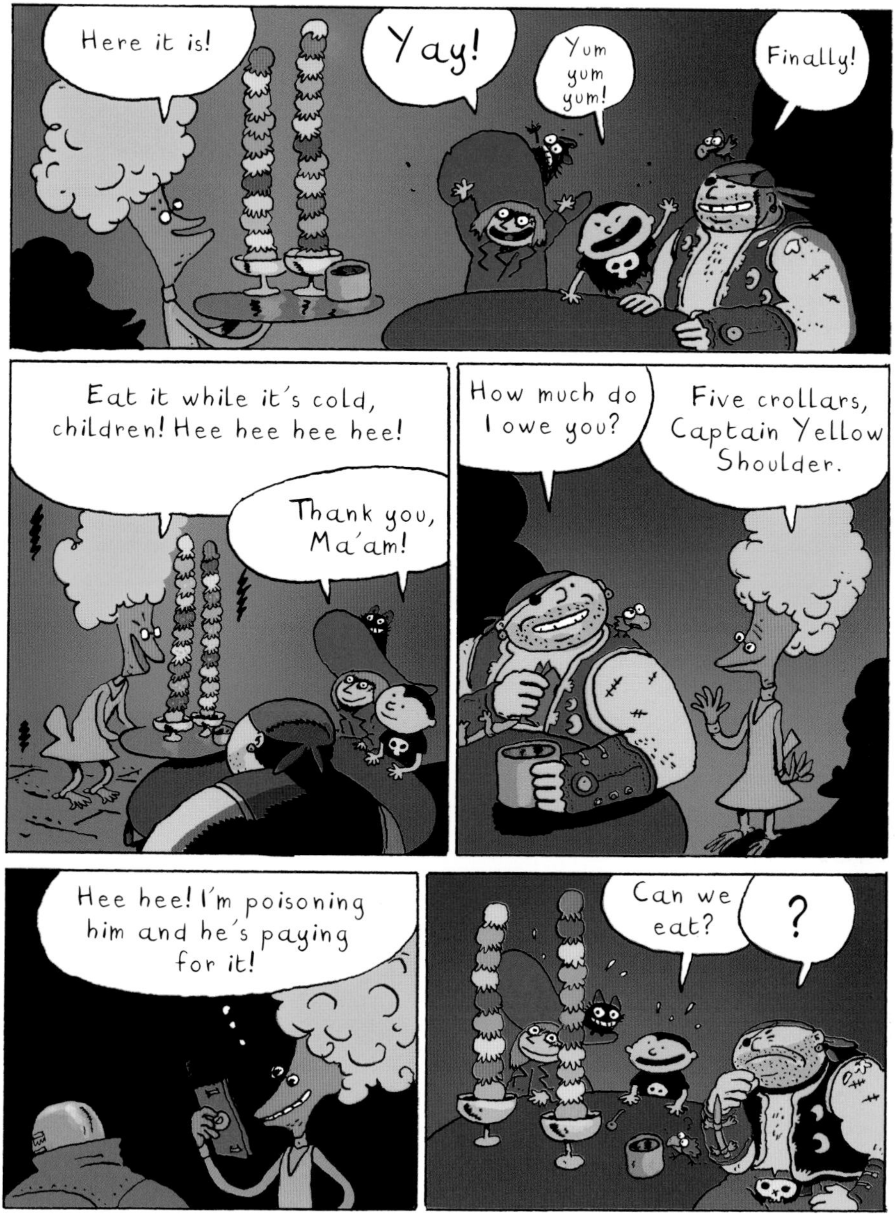
Here it is!
Yay!
Yum yum yum!
Finally!
Eat it while it's cold, children! Hee hee hee hee!
Thank you, Ma'am!
How much do I owe you?
Five crollars, Captain Yellow Shoulder.
Hee hee! I'm poisoning him and he's paying for it!
Can we eat?
?

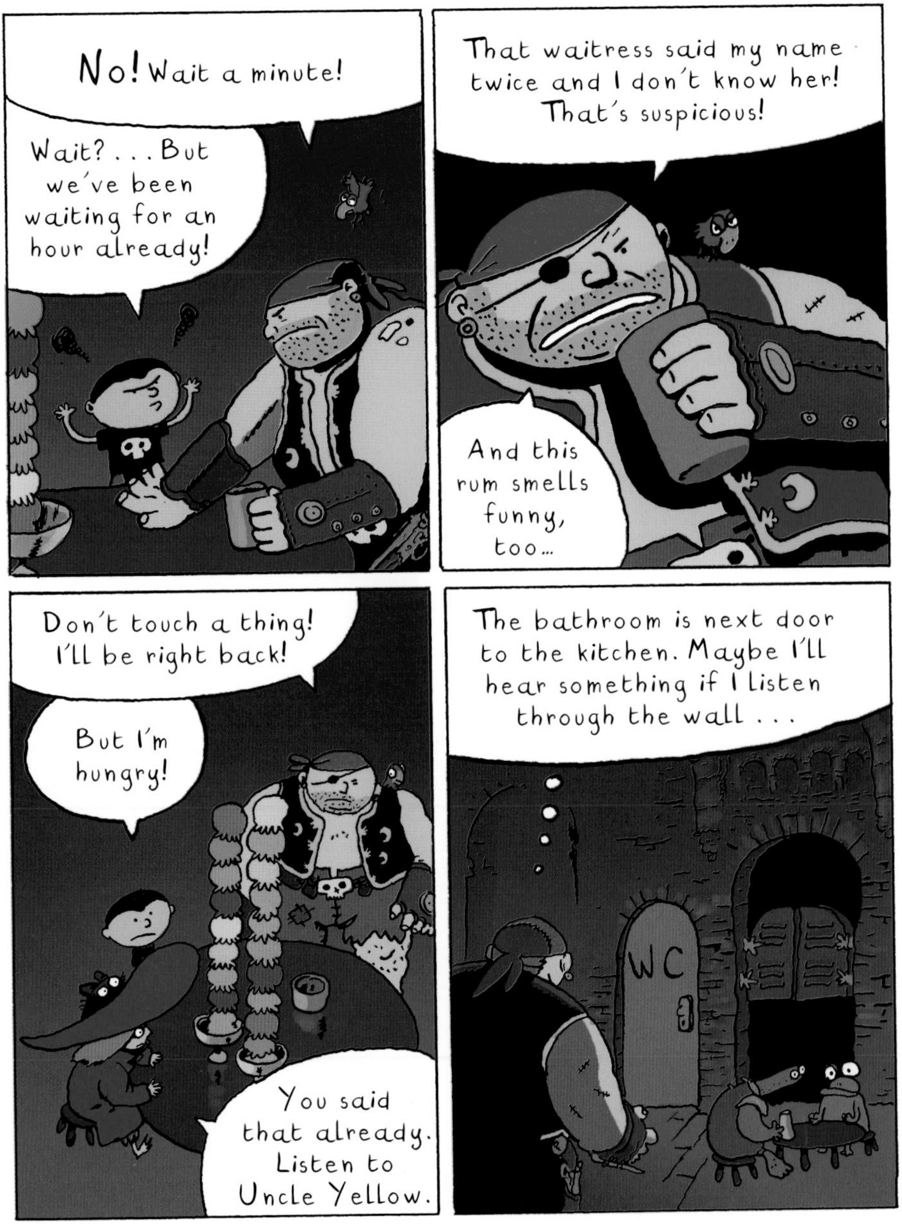
No! Wait a minute!
Wait? . . . But we've been waiting for an hour already!
That waitress said my name twice and I don't know her! That's suspicious!
And this rum smells funny, too...
Don't touch a thing! I'll be right back!
But I'm hungry!
You said that already. Listen to Uncle Yellow.
The bathroom is next door to the kitchen. Maybe I'll hear something if I listen through the wall . . .
WC

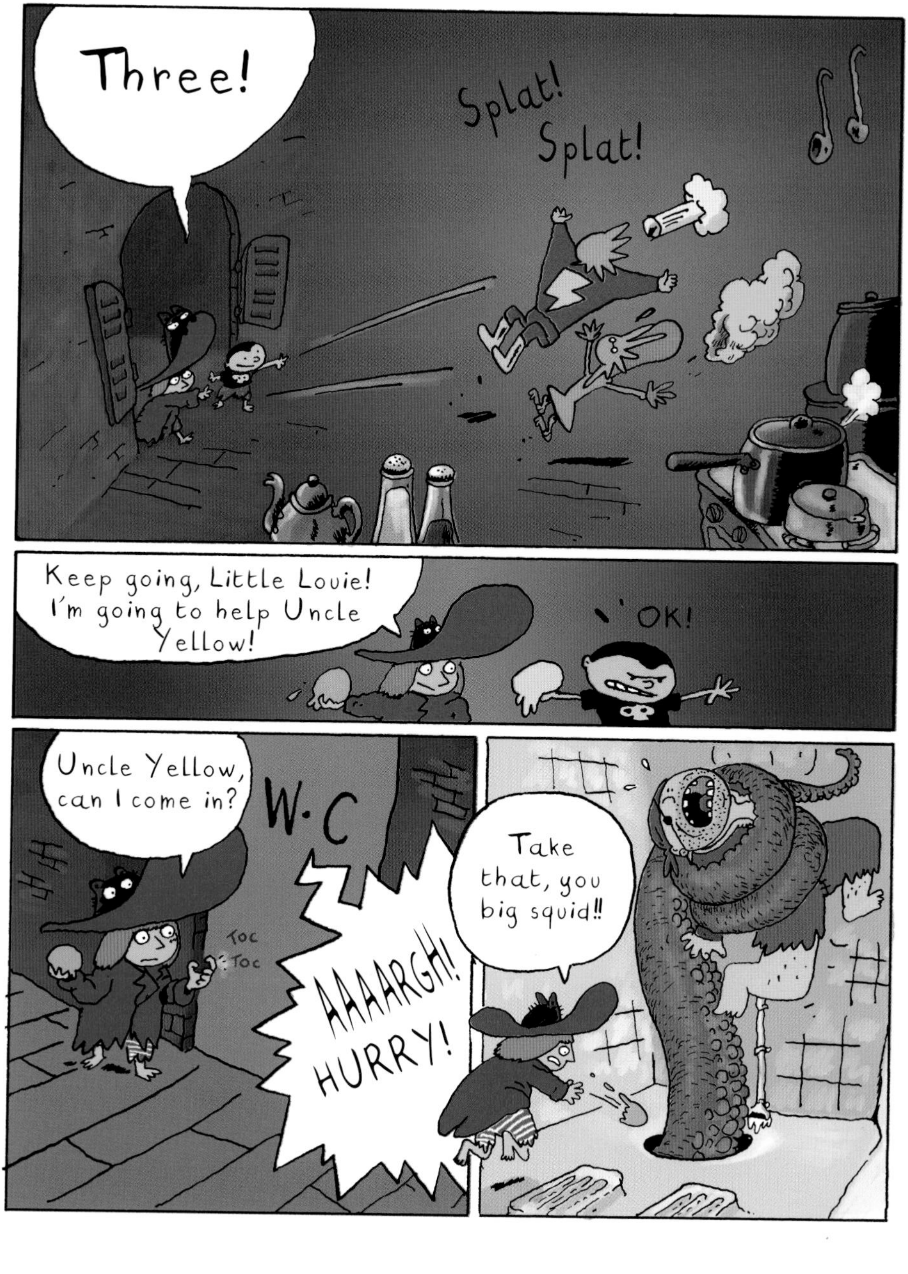
Three!
Splat! Splat!
Keep going, Little Louie! I'm going to help Uncle Yellow!
OK!
Uncle Yellow, can I come in?
W·C
TOC TOC
AAAARGH! HURRY!
Take that, you big squid!!

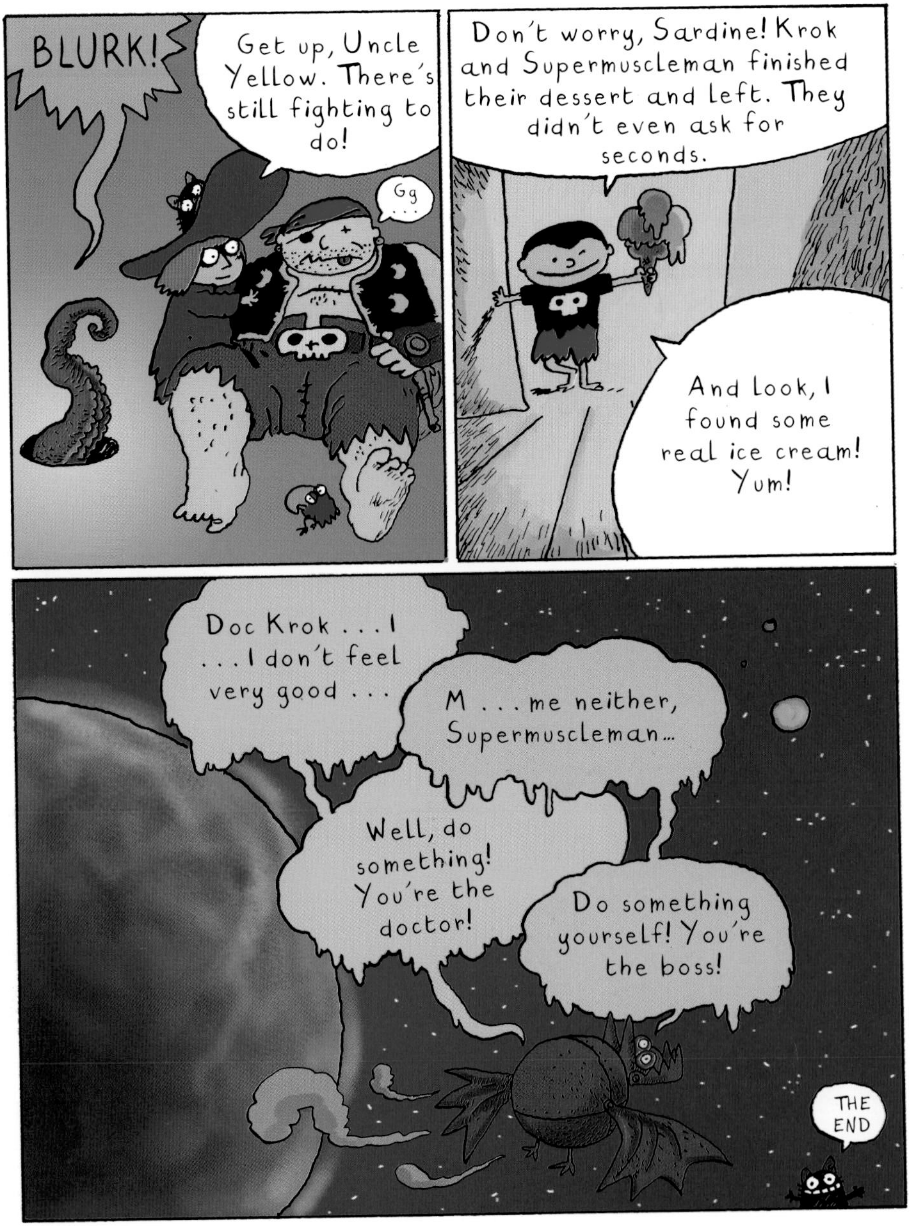
BLURK!
Get up, Uncle Yellow. There's still fighting to do!
Gg . . .
Don't worry, Sardine! Krok and Supermuscleman finished their dessert and left. They didn't even ask for seconds.
And look, I found some real ice cream! Yum!
Doc Krok . . . I . . . I don't feel very good . . .
M . . . me neither, Supermuscleman...
Well, do something! You're the doctor!
Do something yourself! You're the boss!
THE END

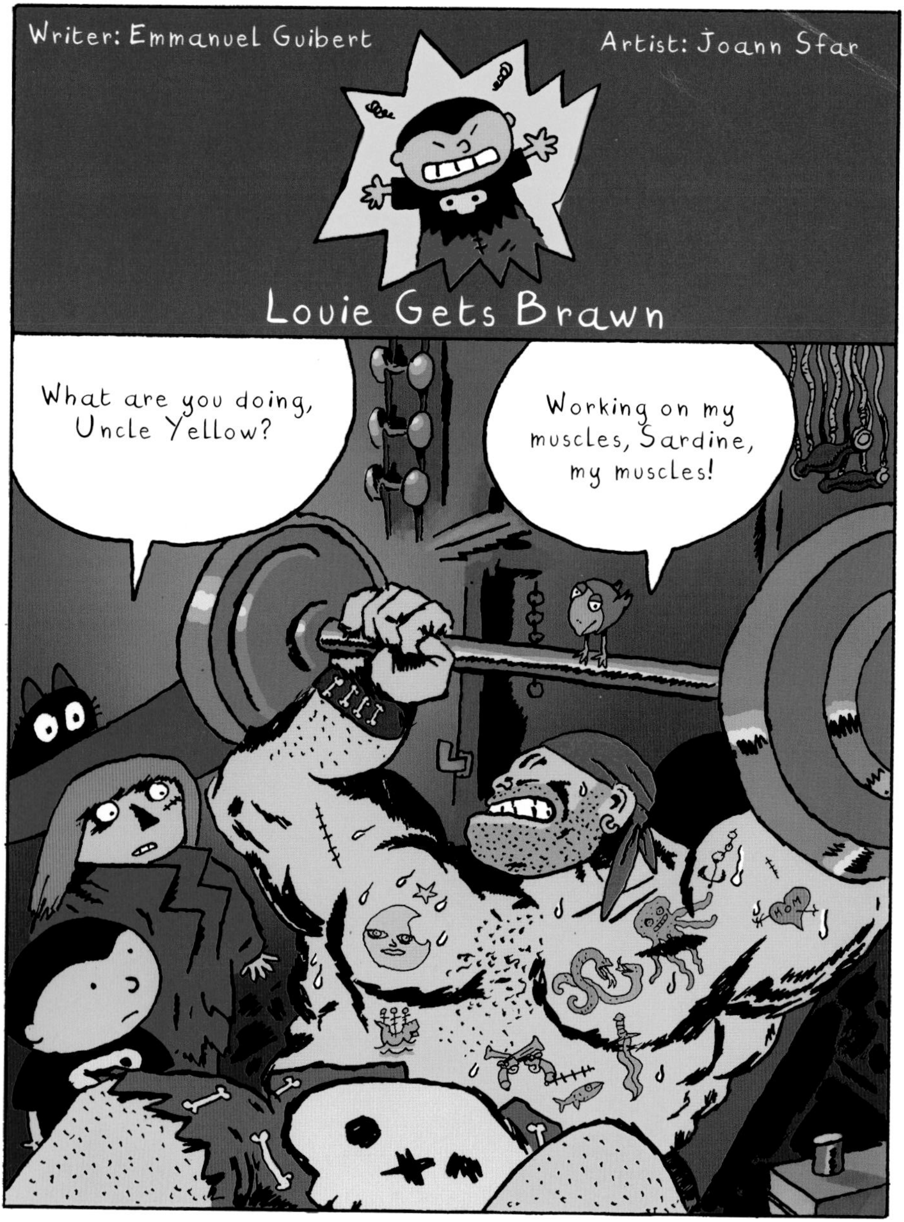

Writer: Emmanuel Guibert
Artist: Joann Sfar
Louie Gets Brawn
What are you doing, Uncle Yellow?
Working on my muscles, Sardine, my muscles!
MOM

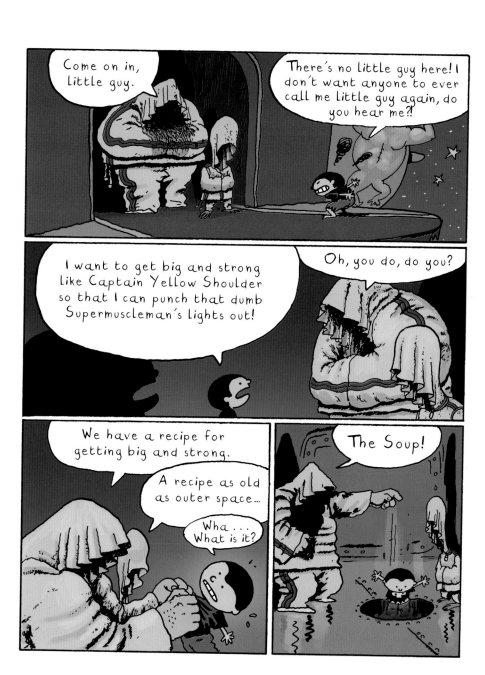

77

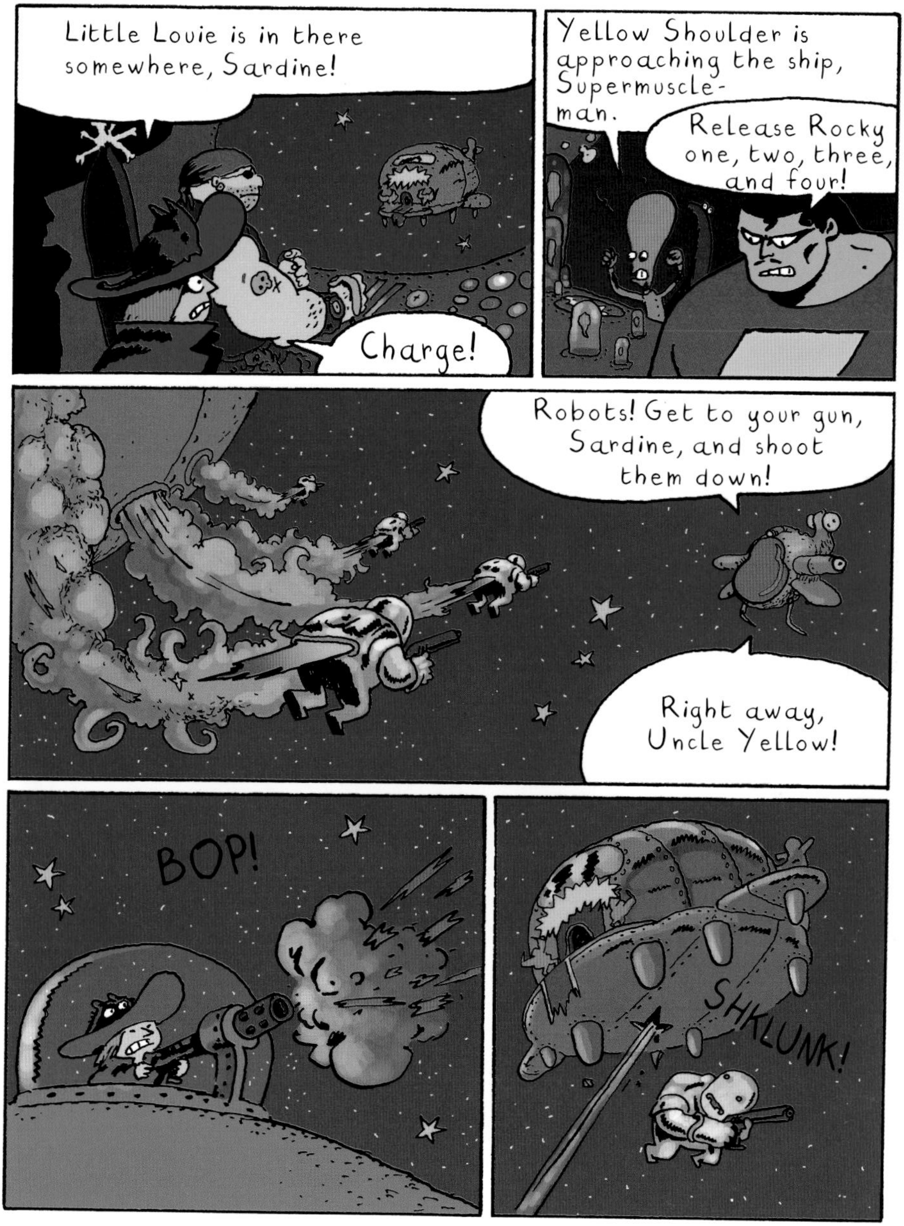
Little Louie is in there somewhere, Sardine!
Charge!
Yellow Shoulder is approaching the ship, Supermuscle-man.
Release Rocky one, two, three, and four!
Robots! Get to your gun, Sardine, and shoot them down!
Right away, Uncle Yellow!
BOP!
SHKLUNK!

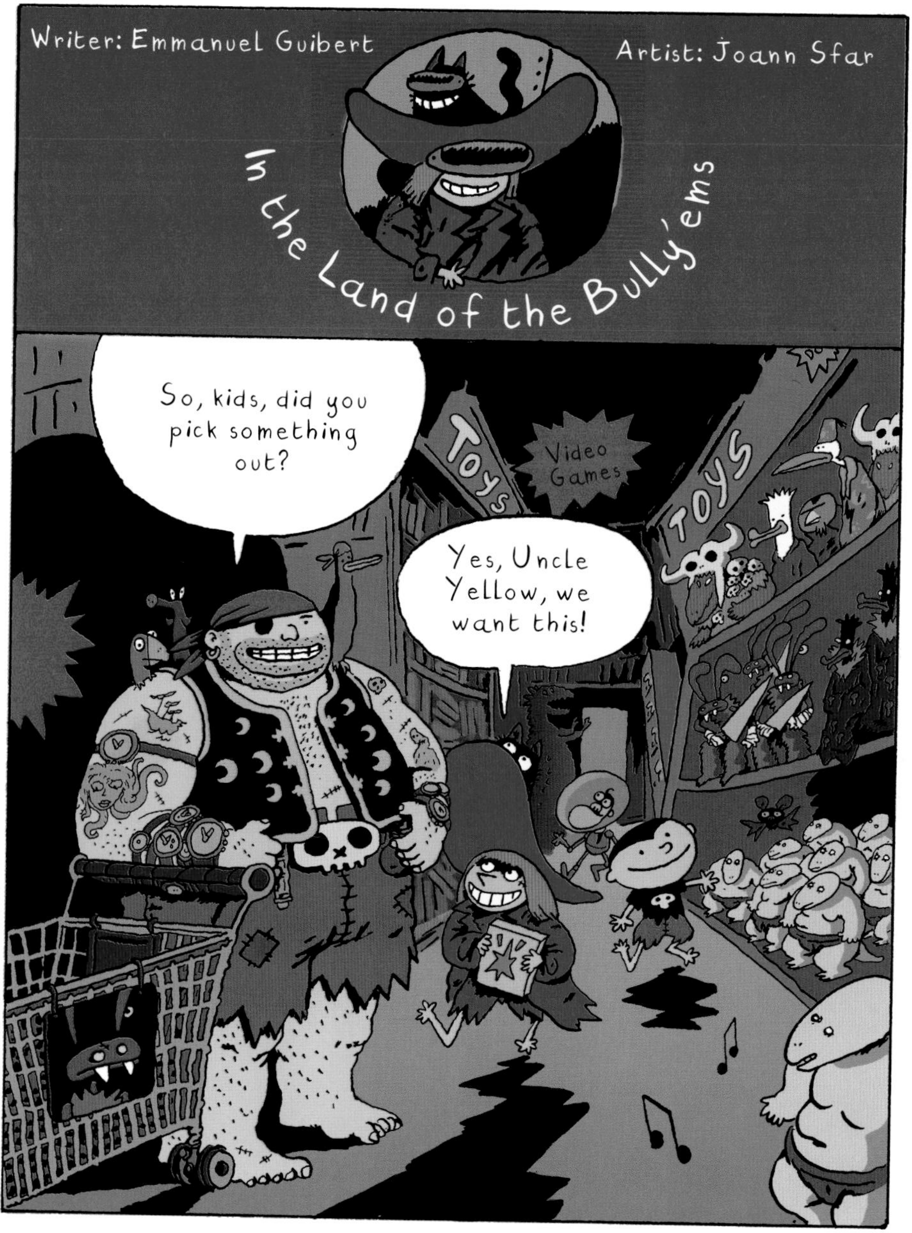
Writer: Emmanuel Guibert
Artist: Joann Sfar
In the Land of the Bully'ems
So, kids, did you pick something out?
Toys
Video Games
TOYS
Yes, Uncle Yellow, we want this!

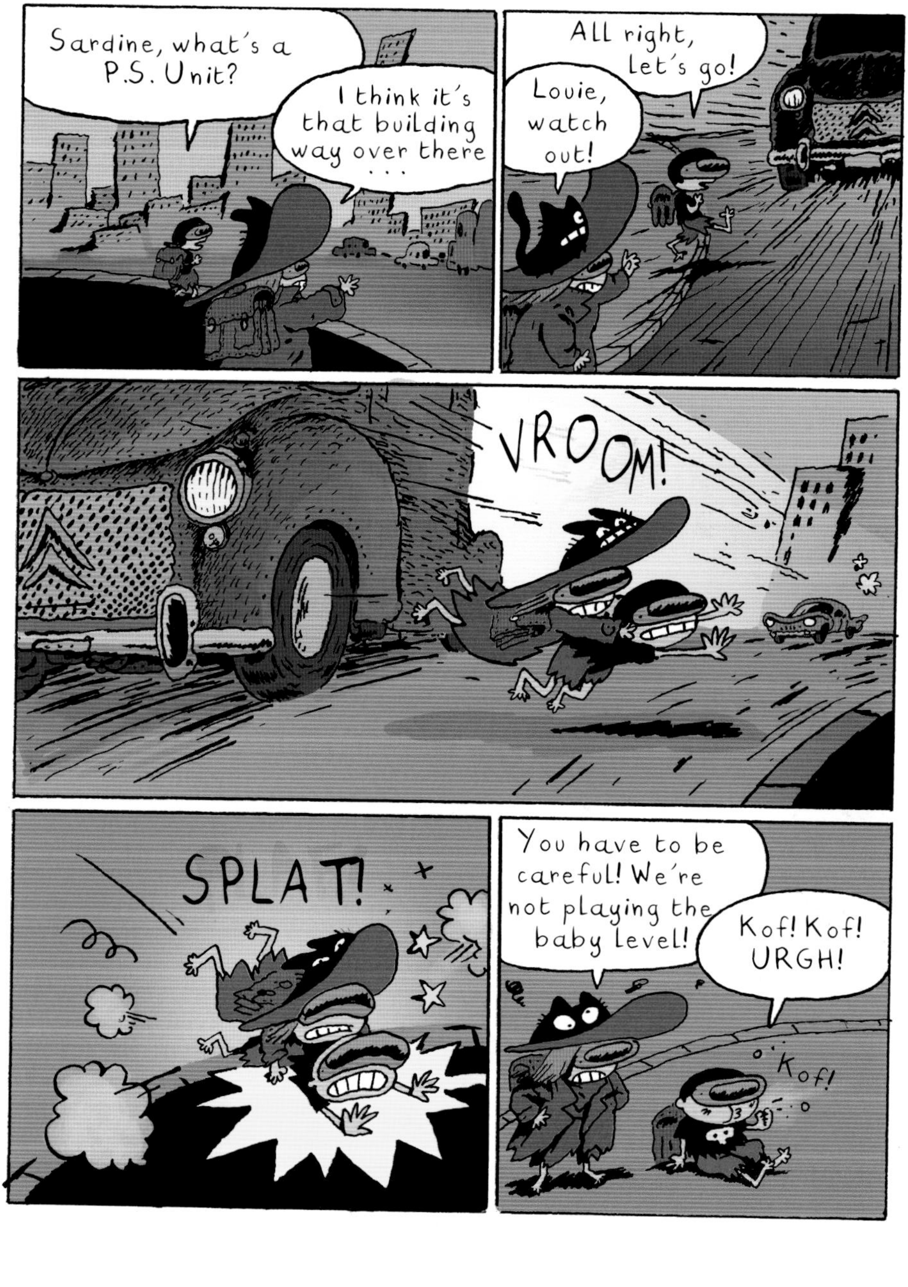
Sardine, what's a P.S. Unit?
I think it's that building way over there . . .
All right, let's go!
Louie, watch out!
VROOM!
SPLAT!
You have to be careful! We're not playing the baby level!
Kof! Kof! URGH!
Kof!

89

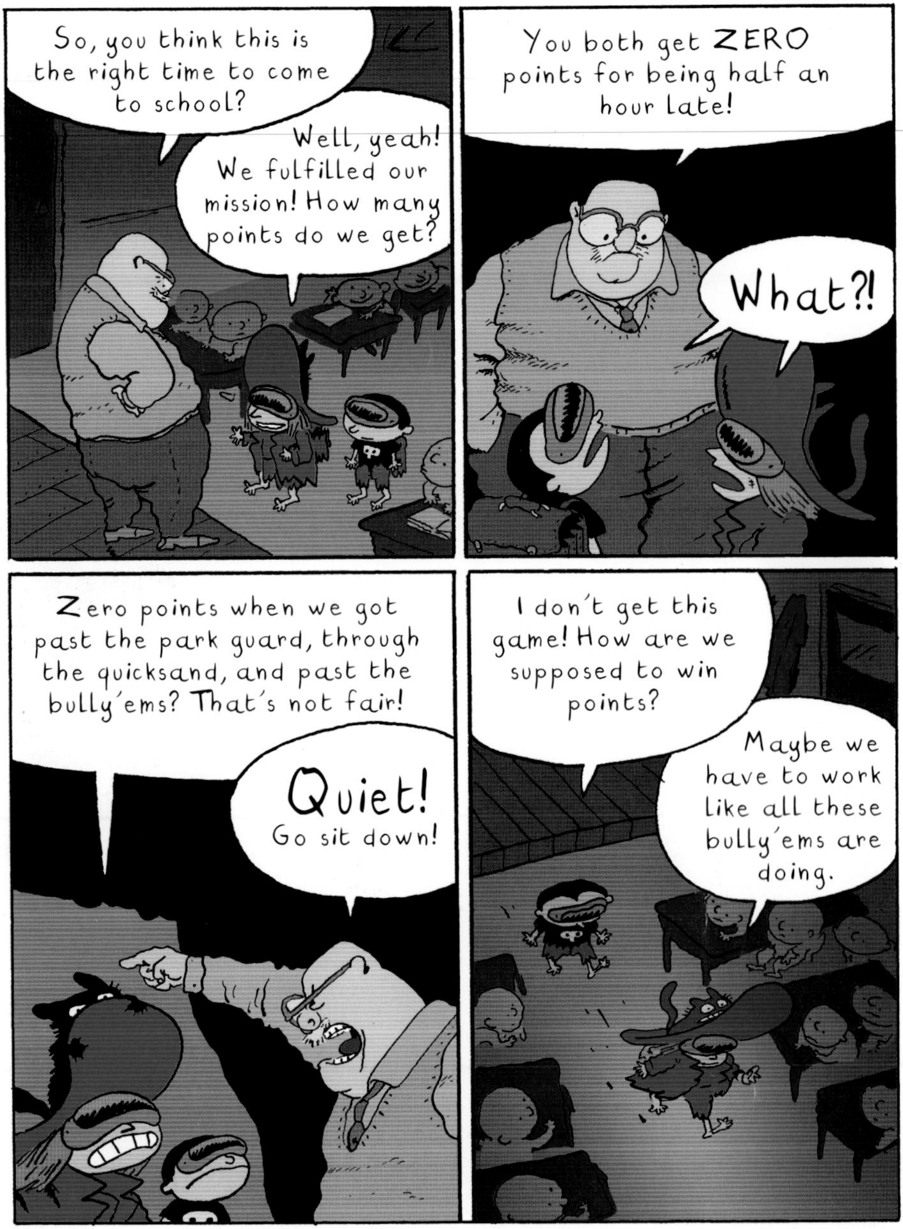
So, you think this is the right time to come to school?
Well, yeah! We fulfilled our mission! How many points do we get?
You both get ZERO points for being half an hour late!
What?!
Zero points when we got past the park guard, through the quicksand, and past the bully'ems? That's not fair!
Quiet! Go sit down!
I don't get this game! How are we supposed to win points?
Maybe we have to work like all these bully'ems are doing.

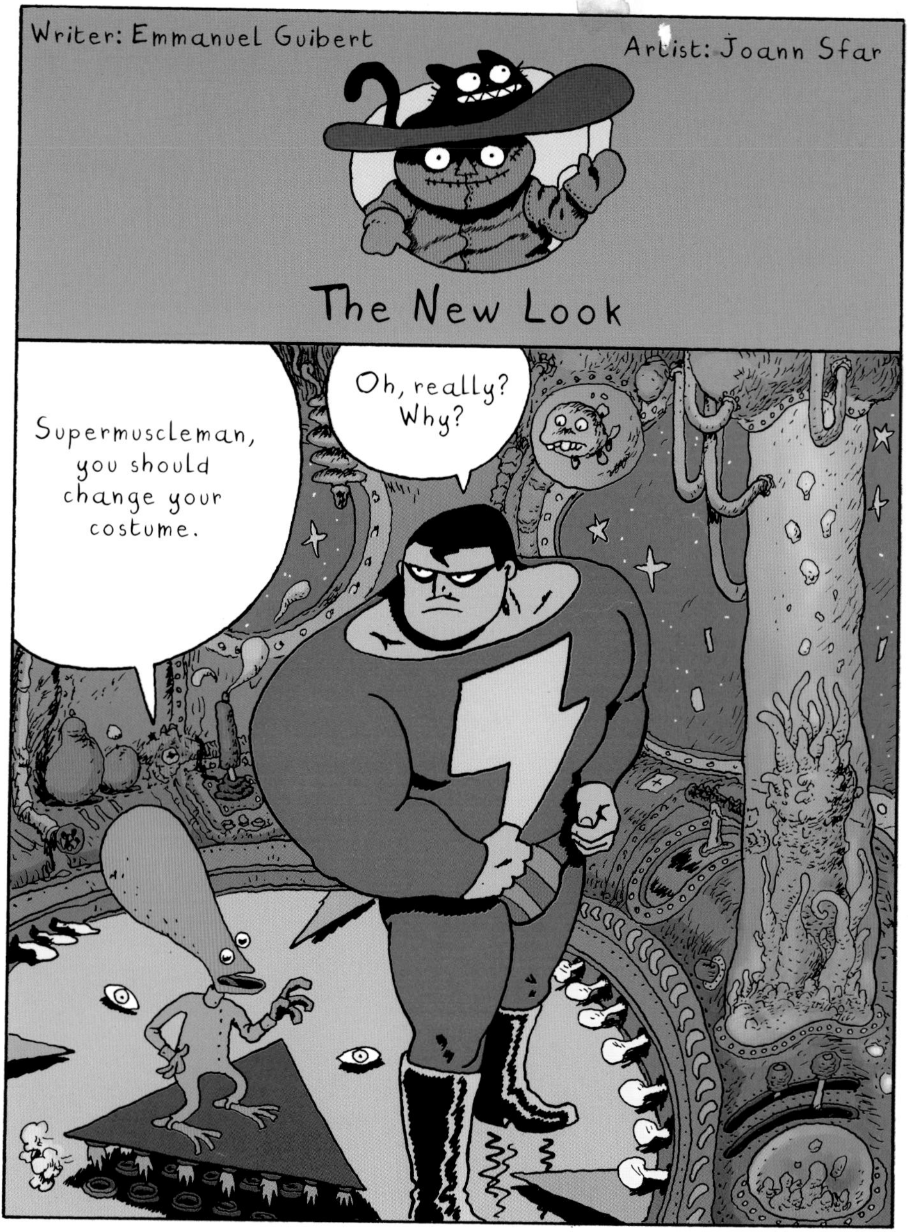
Writer: Emmanuel Guibert
Artist: Joann Sfar
The New Look
Supermuscleman, you should change your costume.
Oh, really? Why?

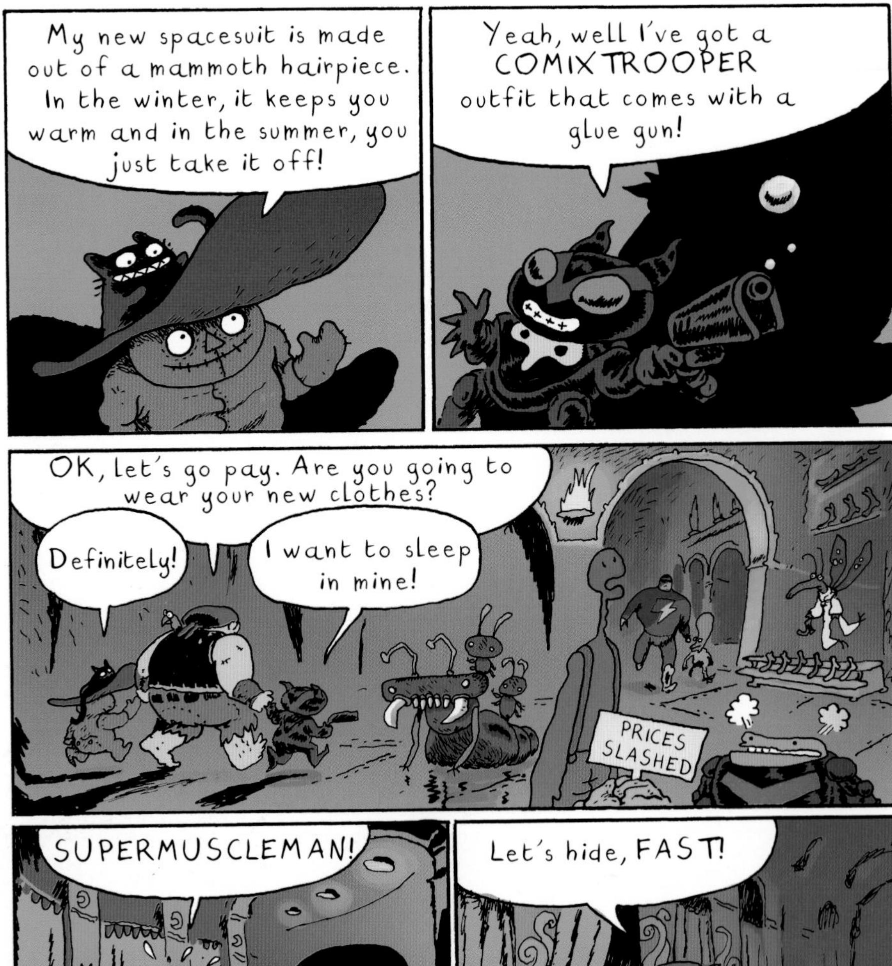
My new spacesuit is made out of a mammoth hairpiece. In the winter, it keeps you warm and in the summer, you just take it off!
Yeah, well I've got a COMIXTROOPER outfit that comes with a glue gun!
OK, let's go pay. Are you going to wear your new clothes?
Definitely!
I want to sleep in mine!
PRICES SLASHED
SUPERMUSCLEMAN!
Let's hide, FAST!

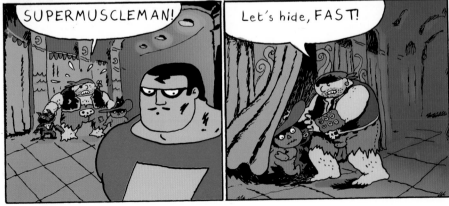

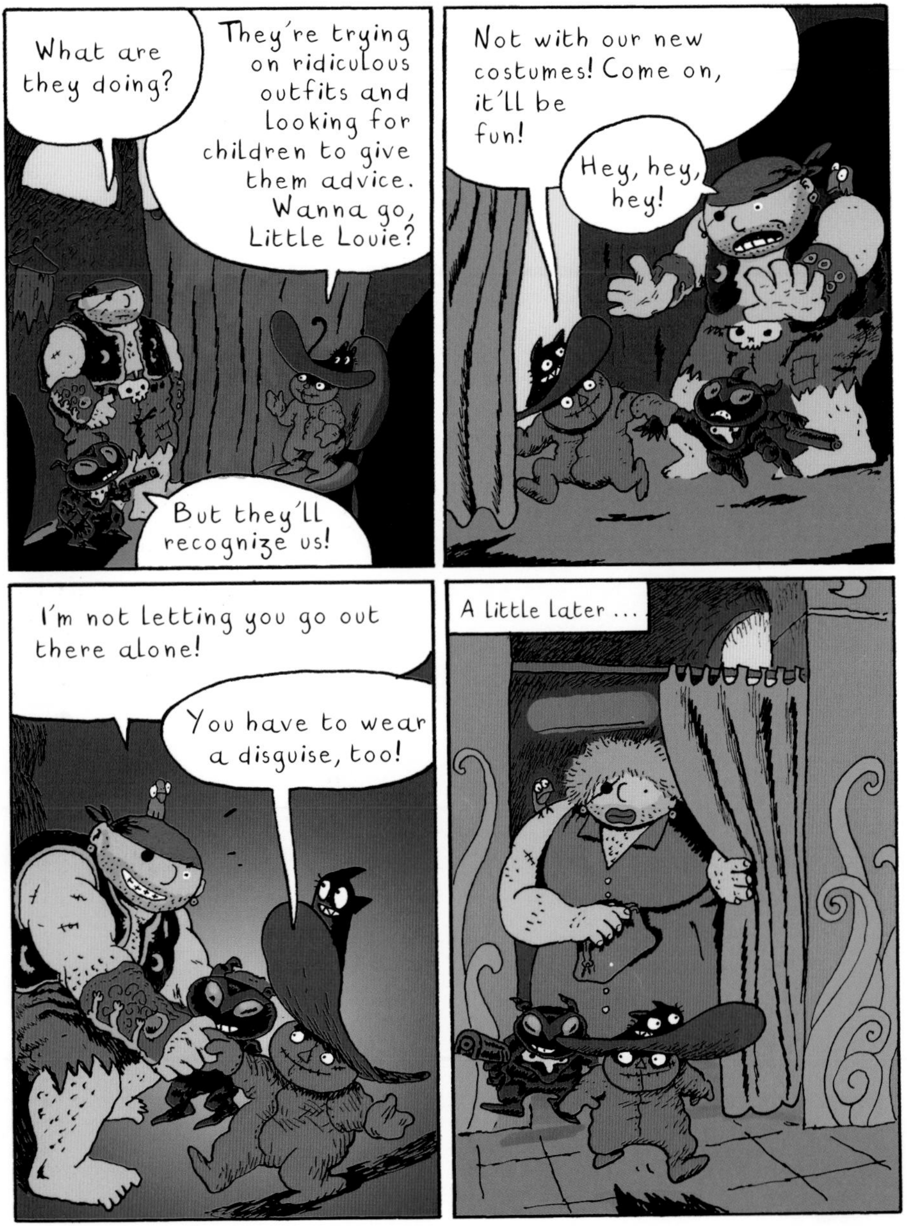
What are they doing?
They're trying on ridiculous outfits and looking for children to give them advice. Wanna go, Little Louie?
But they'll recognize us!
Not with our new costumes! Come on, it'll be fun!
Hey, hey, hey!
I'm not letting you go out there alone!
You have to wear a disguise, too!
A little later ...

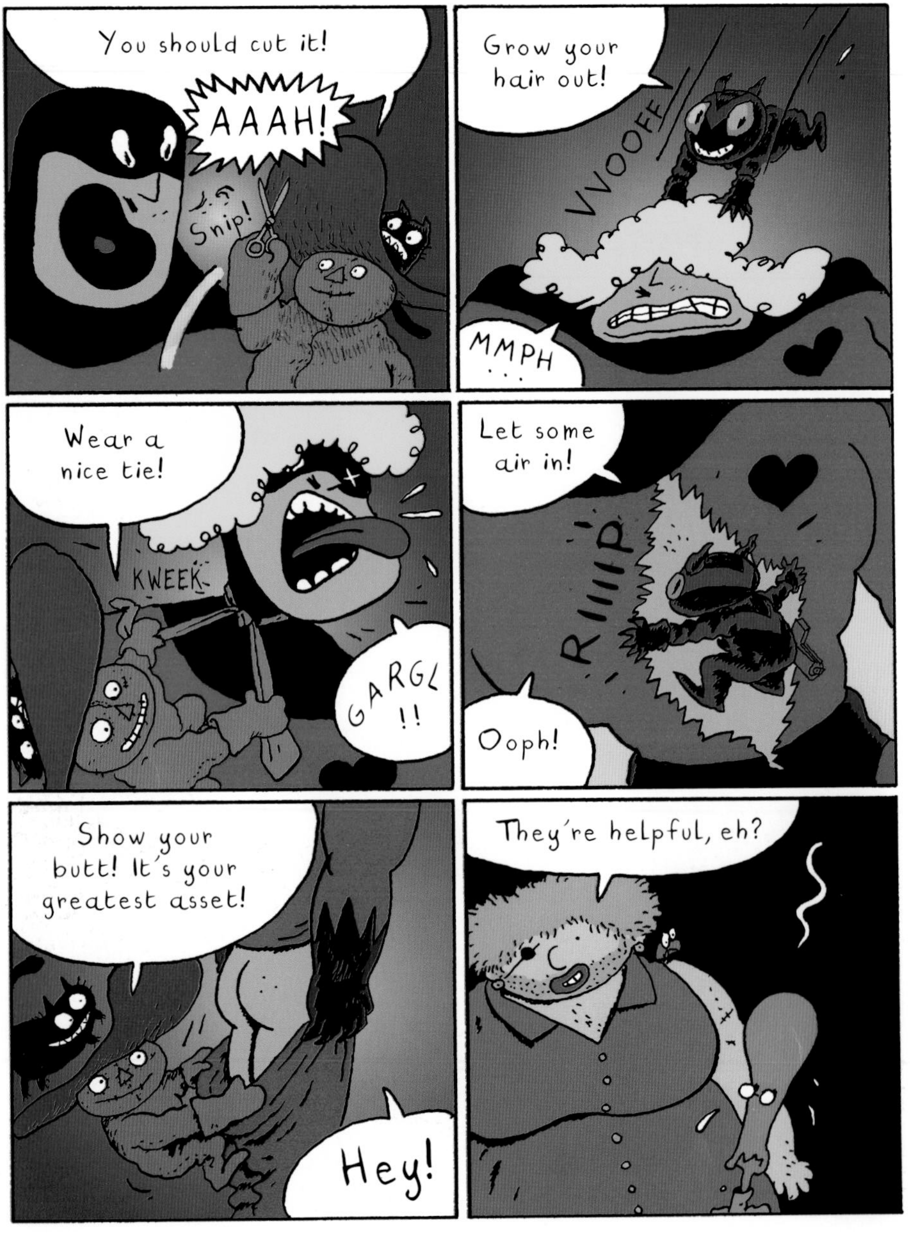
You should cut it!
AAAH!
Snip!
Grow your hair out!
VVOOFF
MMPH...
Wear a nice tie!
KWEEK
GARGL !!
Let some air in!
RIIIIP
Ooph!
Show your butt! It's your greatest asset!
Hey!
They're helpful, eh?

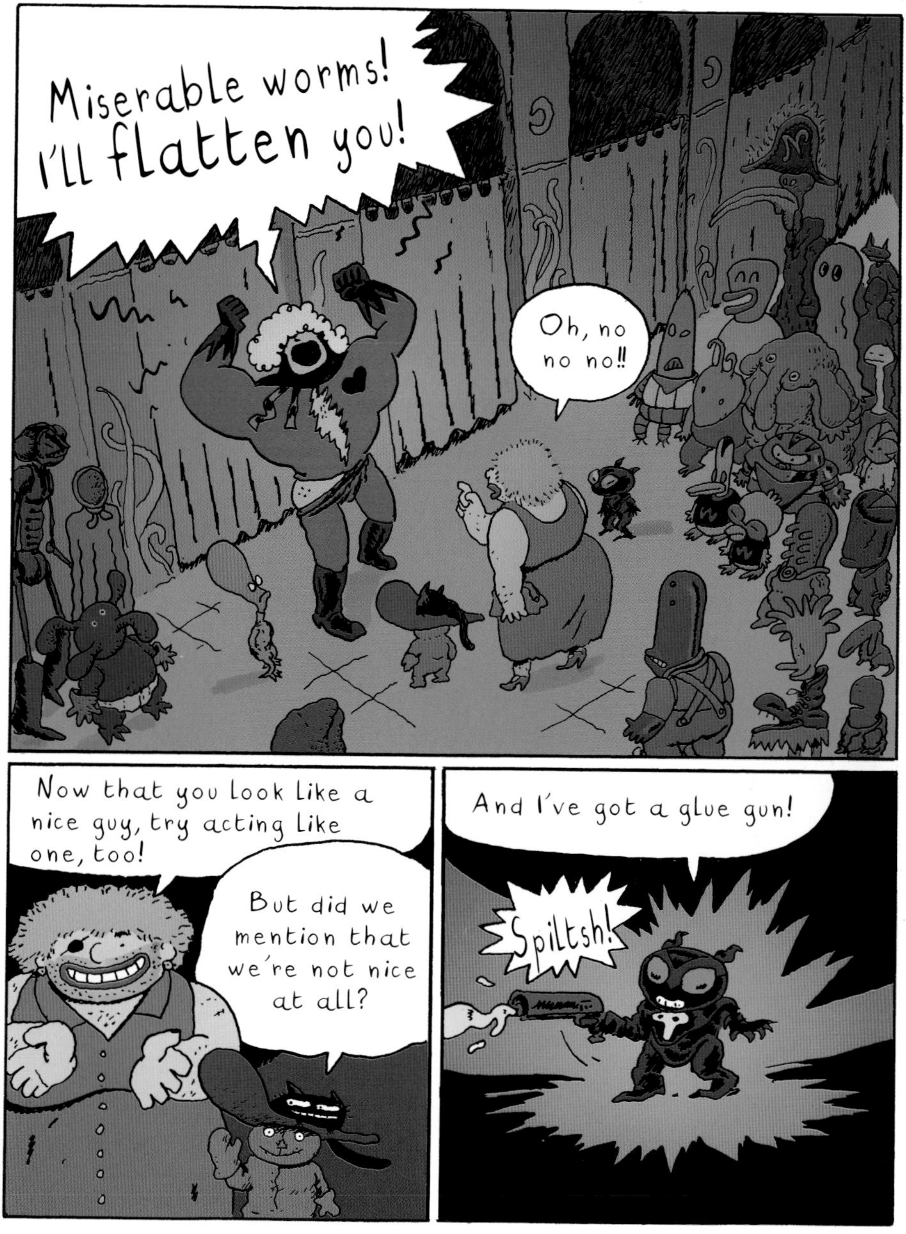
Miserable worms! I'll flatten you!
Oh, no no no!!
Now that you look like a nice guy, try acting like one, too!
But did we mention that we're not nice at all?
And I've got a glue gun!
Spiltsh!

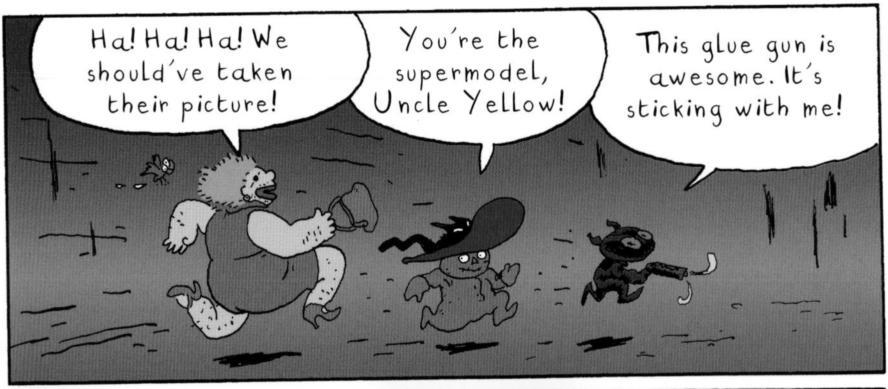
Ha! Ha! Ha! We should've taken their picture!
You're the supermodel, Uncle Yellow!
This glue gun is awesome. It's sticking with me!

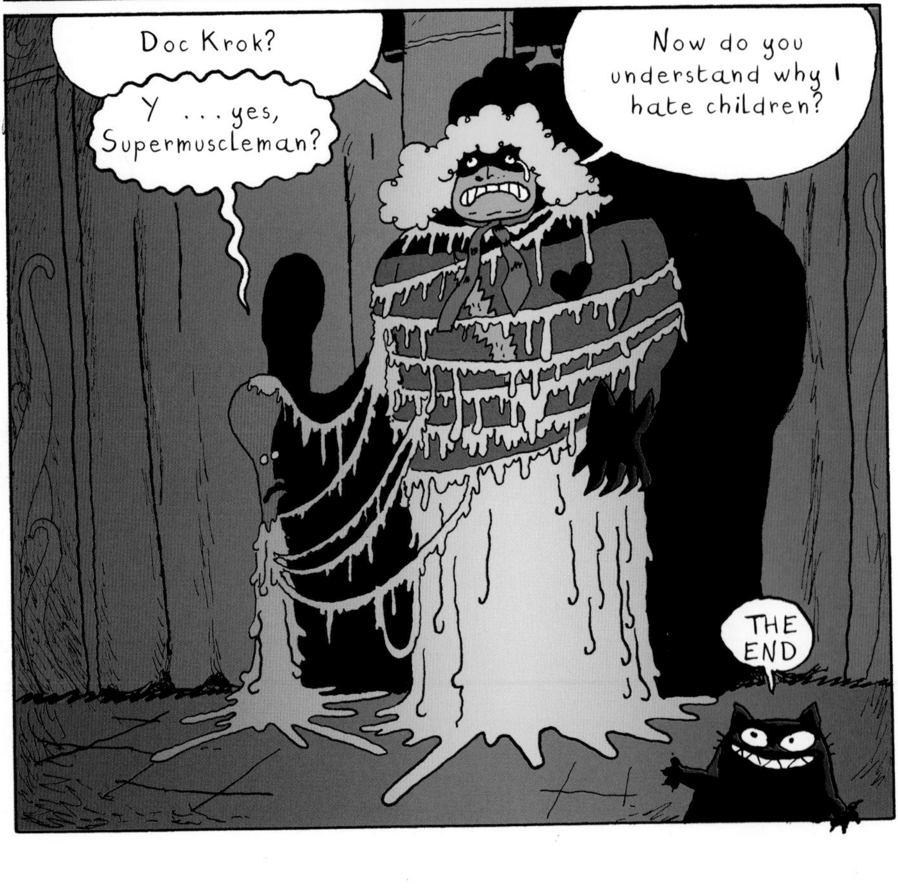
Doc Krok?
Y ...yes, Supermuscleman?
Now do you understand why I hate children?
THE END

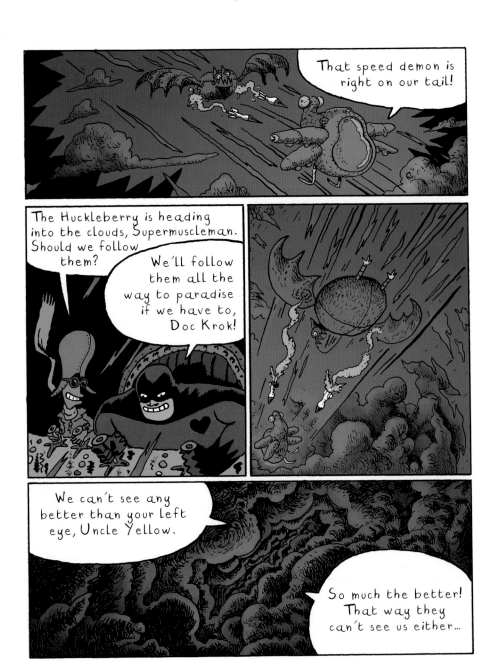

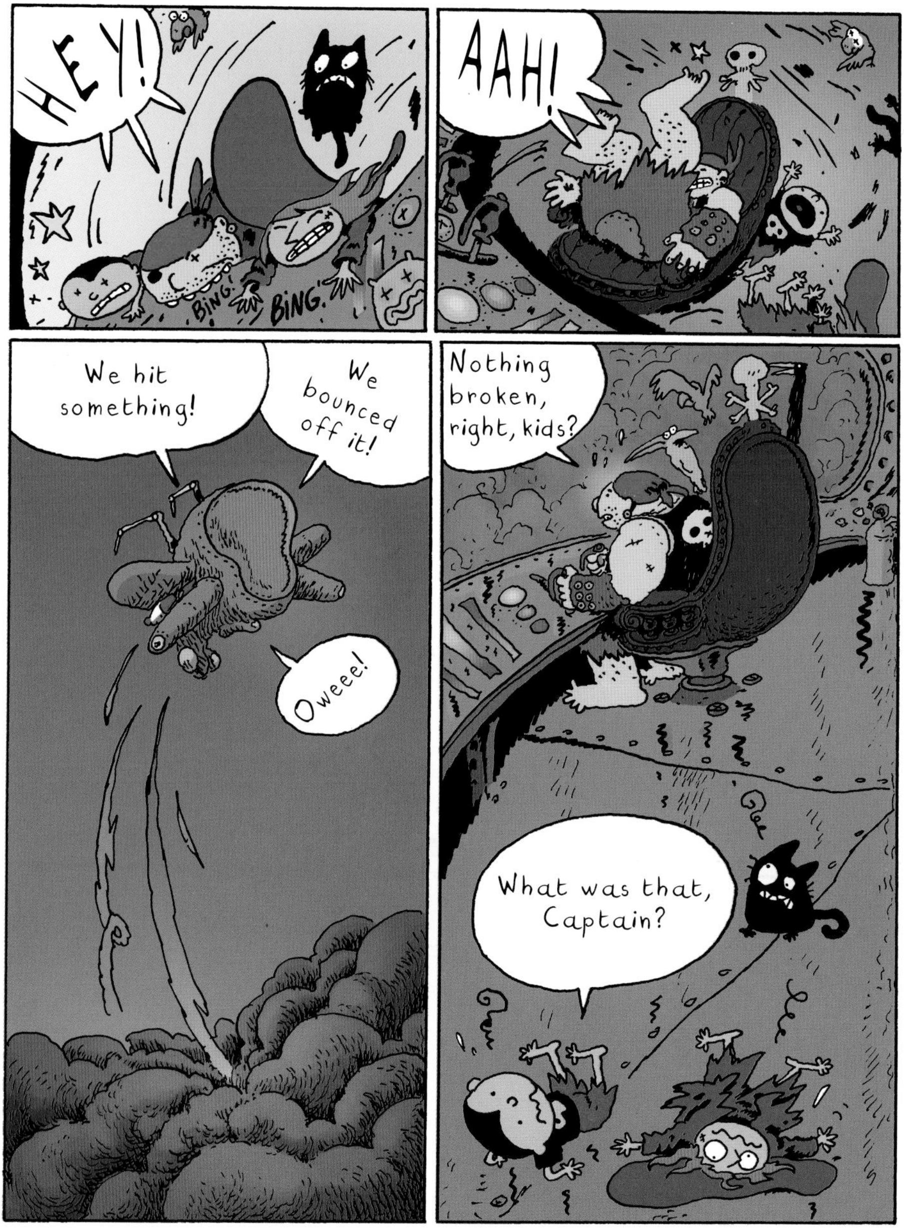
HEY!
BING!
BING!
AAH!
We hit something!
We bounced off it!
Oweee!
Nothing broken, right, kids?
What was that, Captain?

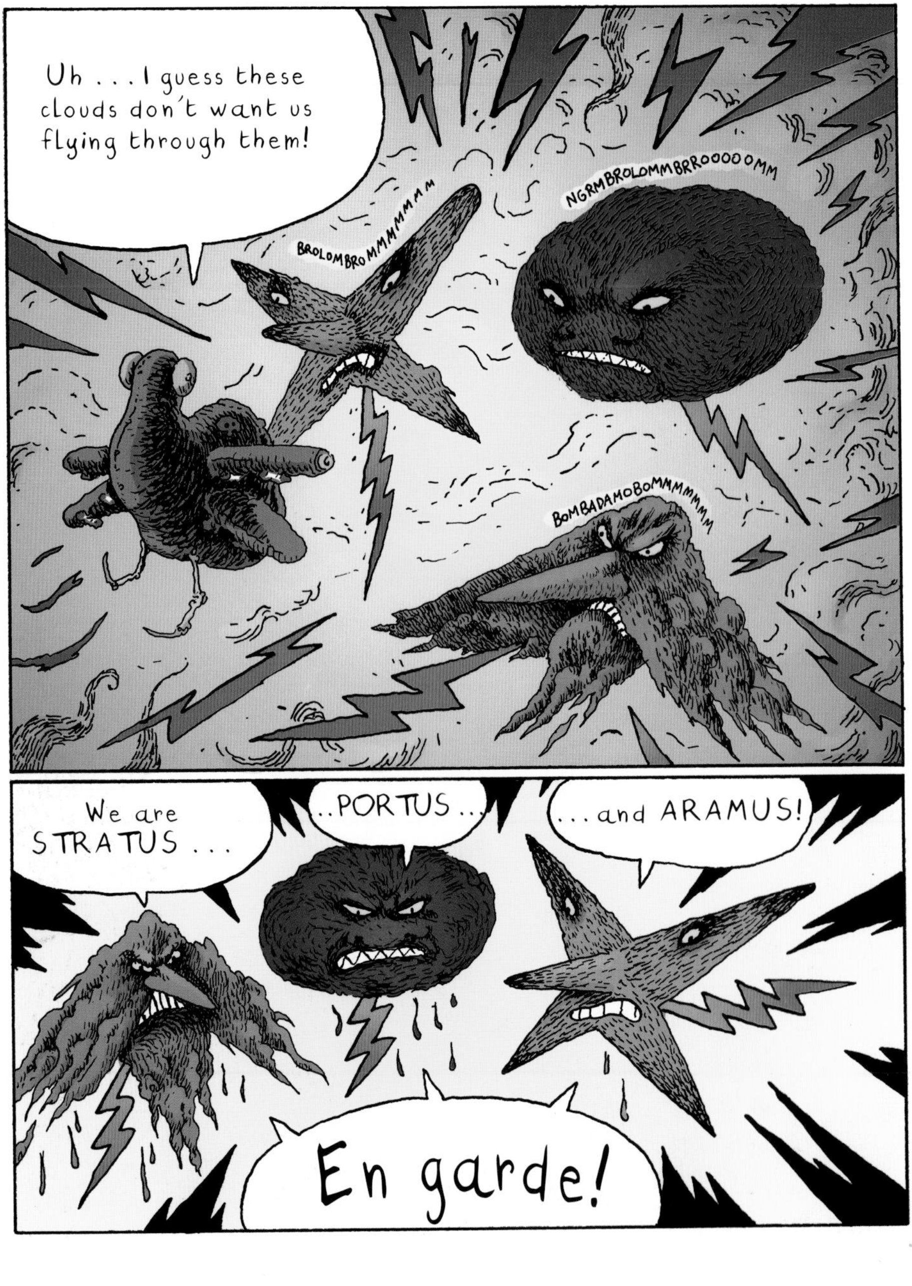
Uh . . . I guess these clouds don't want us flying through them!
BROLOMBROMMMMMM
NGRMBROLOMMBRROOOOOMM
BOMBADAMOBOMMMMMMM
We are STRATUS . . .
. . PORTUS . . .
. . . and ARAMUS!
En garde!

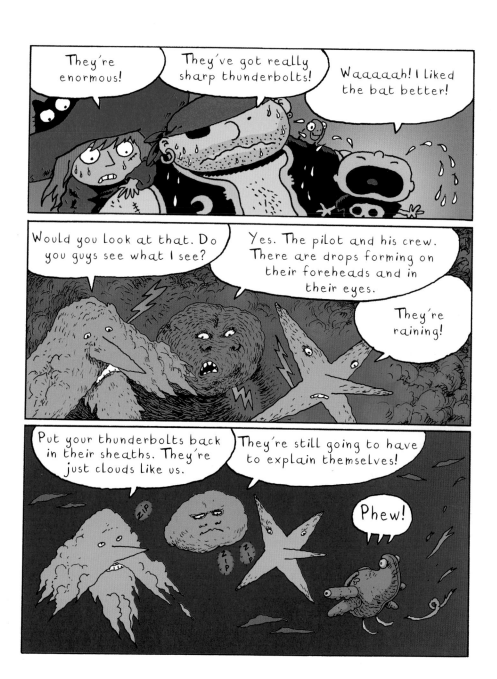

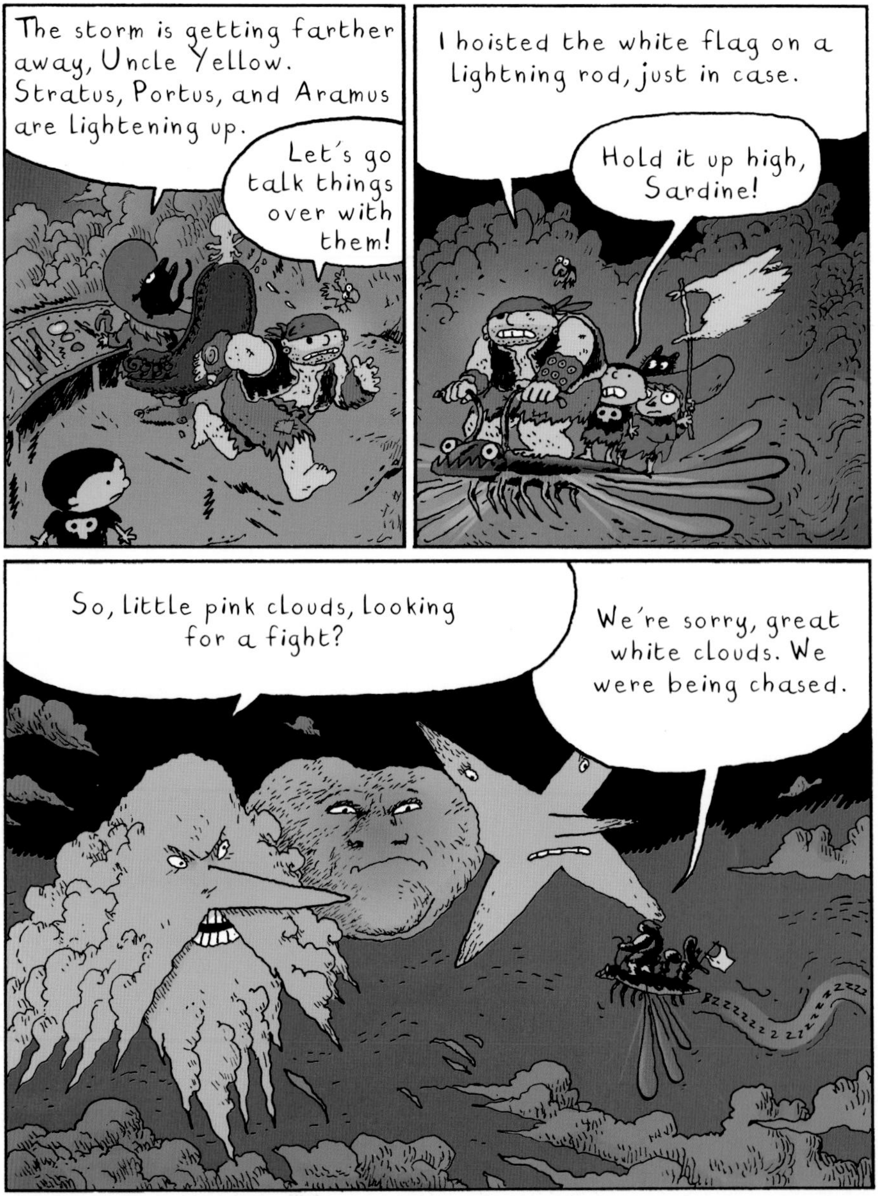
The storm is getting farther away, Uncle Yellow. Stratus, Portus, and Aramus are lightening up.
Let's go talk things over with them!
I hoisted the white flag on a lightning rod, just in case.
Hold it up high, Sardine!
So, little pink clouds, looking for a fight?
We're sorry, great white clouds. We were being chased.
BZZZZZZZZZZZZZZZZZZ

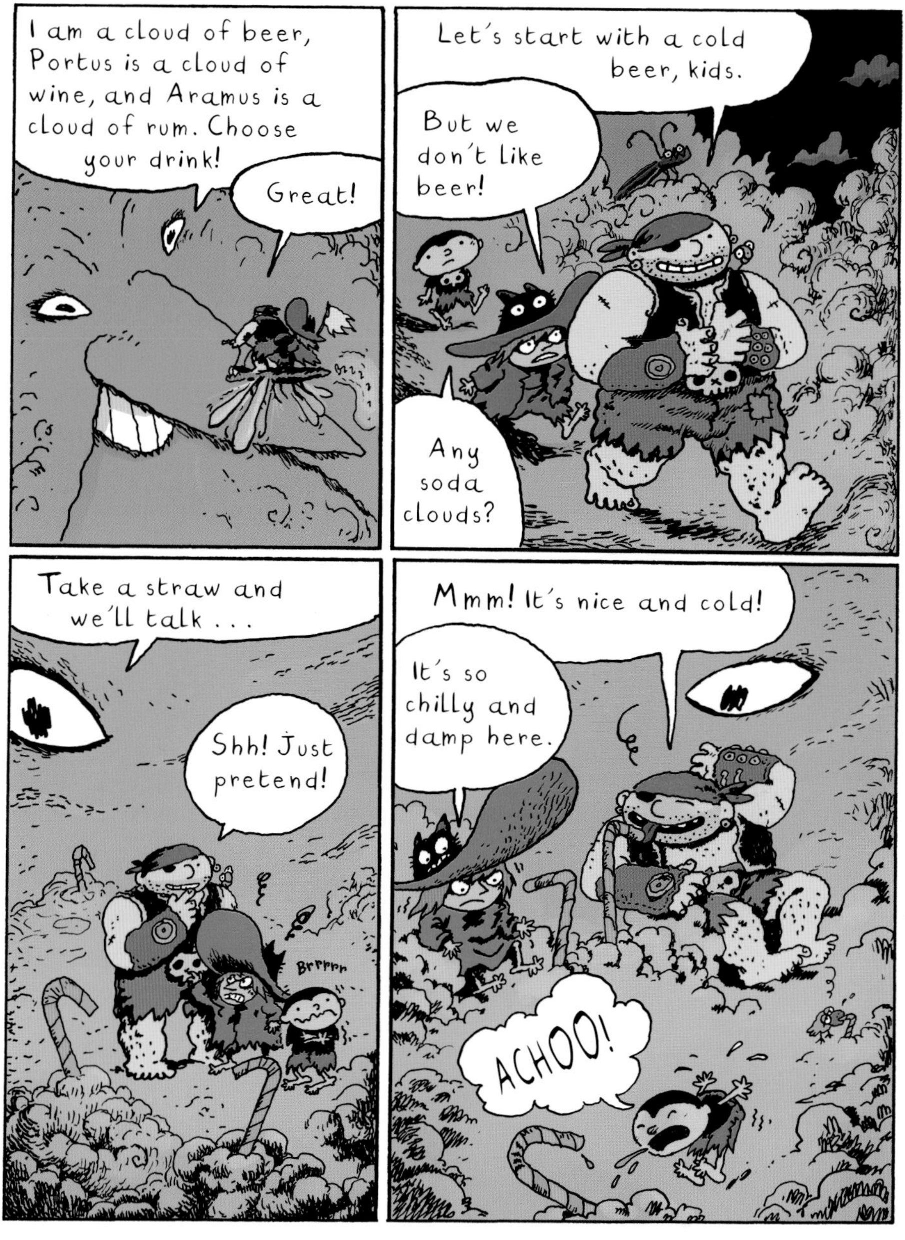
I am a cloud of beer, Portus is a cloud of wine, and Aramus is a cloud of rum. Choose your drink!
Great!
Let's start with a cold beer, kids.
But we don't like beer!
Any soda clouds?
Take a straw and we'll talk . . .
Shh! Just pretend!
Brrrrr
Mmm! It's nice and cold!
It's so chilly and damp here.
ACHOO!

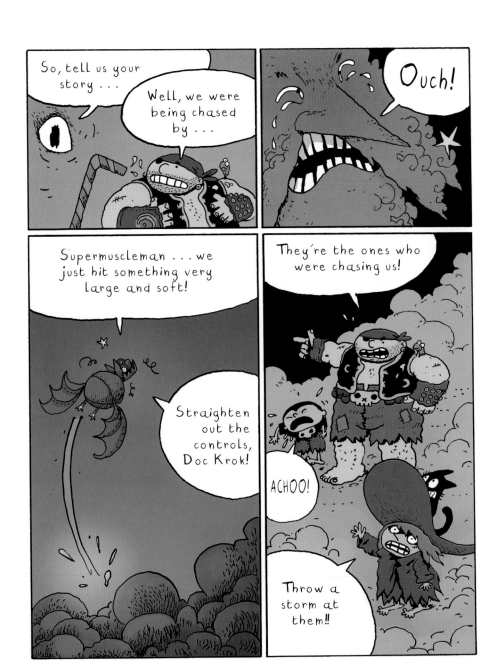

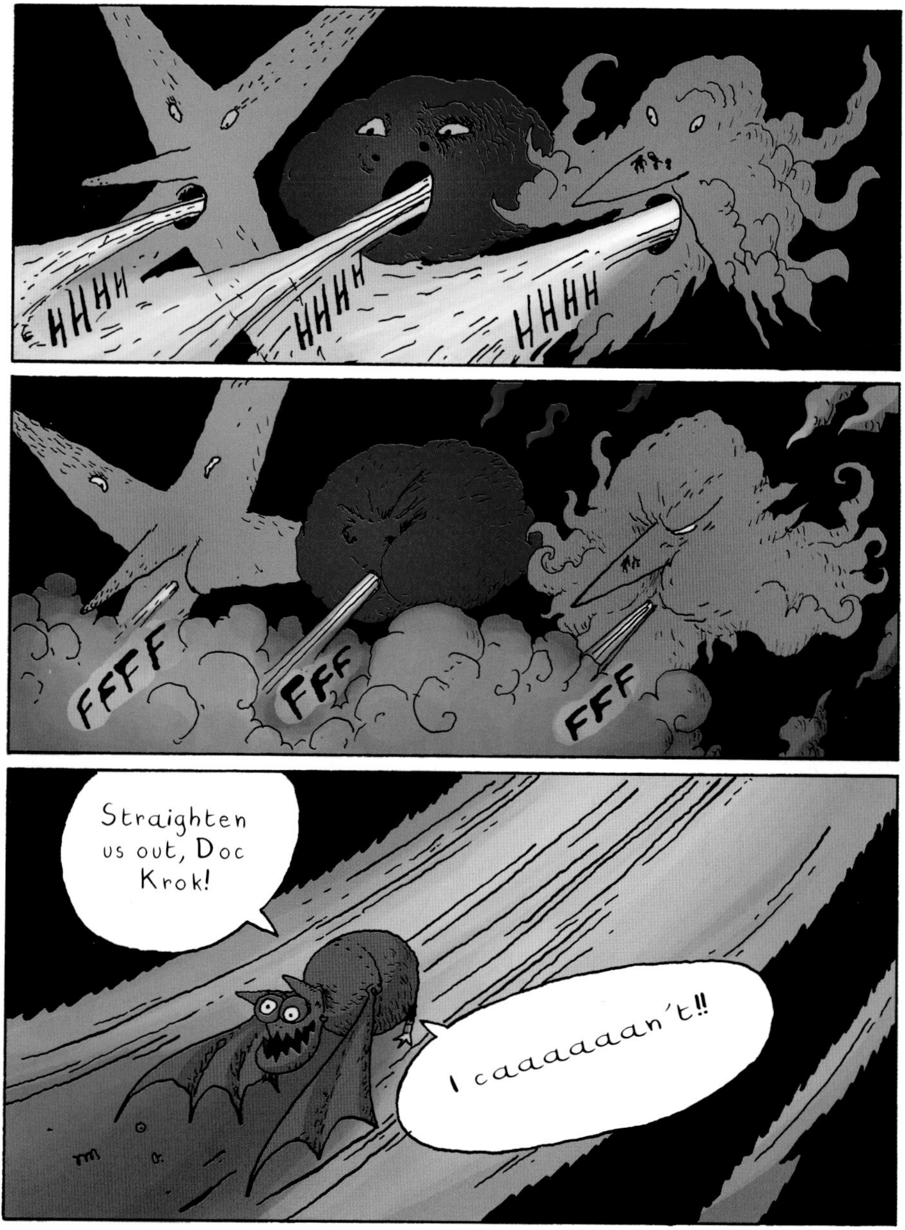
HHHH
HHHH
HHHH
FFFF
FFF
FFF
Straighten us out, Doc Krok!
I caaaaaan't!!

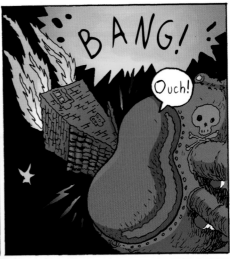

115

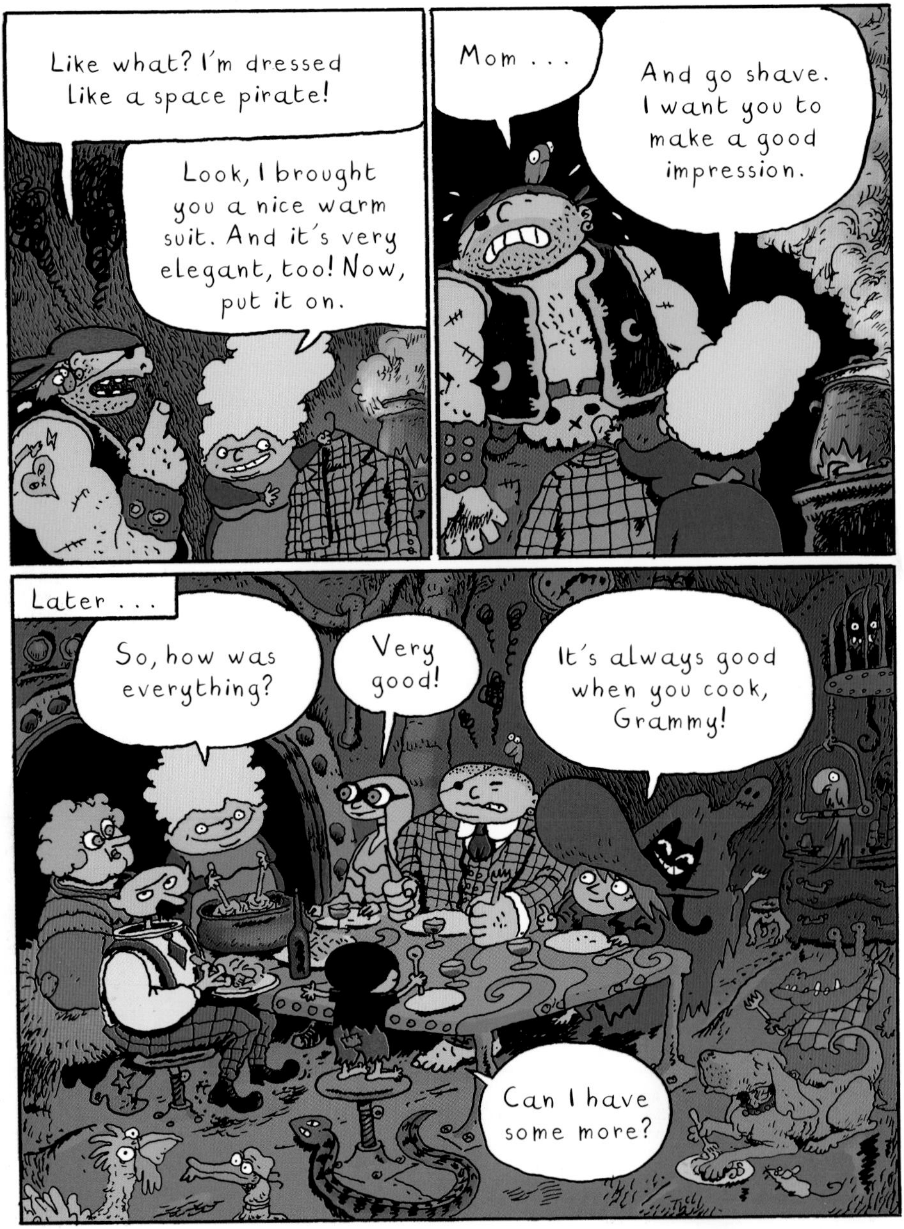
Like what? I'm dressed like a space pirate!
Look, I brought you a nice warm suit. And it's very elegant, too! Now, put it on.
Mom . . .
And go shave. I want you to make a good impression.
Later . . .
So, how was everything?
Very good!
It's always good when you cook, Grammy!
Can I have some more?

119

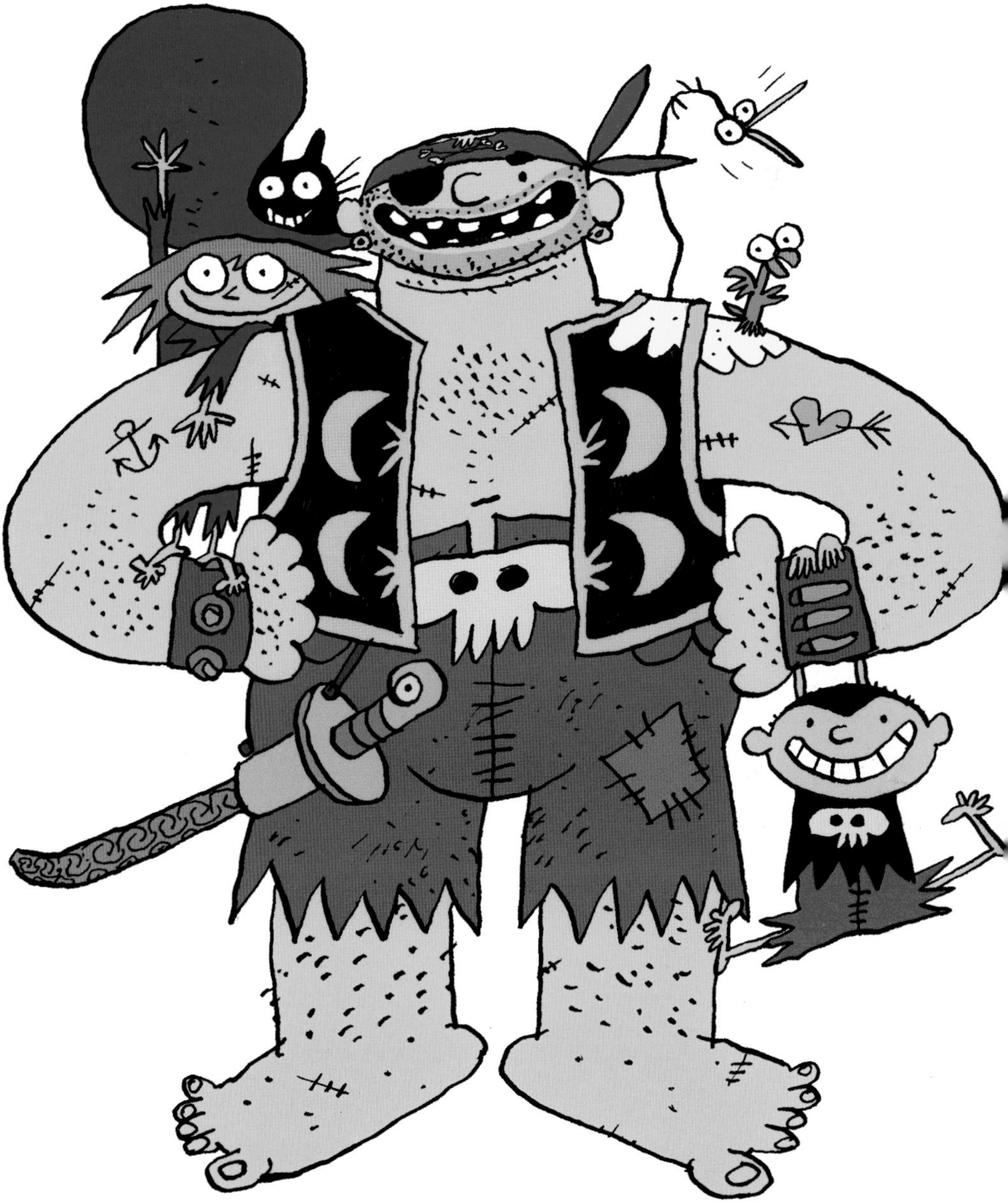